# The Eerie Canal

## by Jack Reber

**Royal Fireworks Press**

Unionville, New York

Copyright © 1996, R Fireworks Publishing Company, Ltd.
All Rights Reserved.

Originally published in 1991 by Trillium Press, Inc.

Royal Fireworks Press
First Avenue, PO Box 399
Unionville, NY 10988
(845) 726-4444
FAX (845) 726-3824
email: rfpress@frontiernet.net
ISBN:     0-89824-996-1  Paperback
          0-89824-997-X  Library Edition


Printed in the United States of America using vegetable-based inks on
acid-free, recycled paper by the Royal Fireworks Printing Co. of
Unionville, New York.

# TABLE OF CONTENTS

| | | |
|---|---|---|
| 1 | An Unusual Field Trip | 1 |
| 2 | All Dressed Up | 8 |
| 3 | Changing Mules | 14 |
| 4 | Rebecca Gets Her Wish | 18 |
| 5 | Hoggee Lessons | 24 |
| 6 | Making Peace | 30 |
| 7 | Grave Robbers | 35 |
| 8 | A Secret Is Discovered | 42 |
| 9 | The Caterpillar Race | 48 |
| 10 | Polly's Present | 53 |
| 11 | Letters and Checkers | 58 |
| 12 | Breach | 64 |
| 13 | Showing Off | 69 |
| 14 | First Aid | 77 |
| 15 | Dr. Evans' Cure | 82 |
| 16 | At the Genesee Falls | 91 |
| 17 | Sam's Leap | 97 |
| 18 | Home at Last? | 103 |

# DEDICATION

In the tradition of canalboat captains, I named the canalboat in this novel for my wife Lenore and my daughter Annie.

In appreciation for their help and support, I dedicate this book to them as well.

# THANK YOU

To the Erie Canal Museum, 318 Erie Blvd., East, Syracuse, New York for the illustrations in this book.

# CHAPTER ONE

# An Unusual Field Trip

Tom Lenhart glared angrily at the two boys. He stood apart from his fourth grade classmates, who had gathered in a group next to the schoolbus. It was a sunny and warm November day, perfect for the first field trip of the school year. Tom didn't feel sunny and warm though. He wanted to hit somebody and he knew the perfect choices, Danny Watson and Jason Reilly. They had kicked the back of his seat for what seemed like the whole bus ride.

Mrs. Ferguson, their teacher, was waiting for the roar of an airplane passing overhead to stop so that she could give instructions. Danny and Jason stared back at Tom. "As you know, we are visiting this park so that you can see what the old Erie Canal was like," began Mrs. Ferguson.

"We've been studying the canal in class, but it's more interesting if you see it for yourself. Does anyone remember how big the canal was?"

"It was 40 feet wide and four feet deep," answered Sandy Jenkins, the class brain.

"Right, Sandy. If you look behind me you can see for yourselves the actual size of the canal. Not very big for such an important achievement, is it? Okay, there's two things to do before lunch. You can go down the path to the right with Mrs. Crawford, our homeroom mother. That path leads to an old dry dock where they used to repair canalboats. The other choice is to follow me up the path to the left and visit an old lock. Keep safety in mind and be back here at 11:30 so that we can eat lunch. Lock visitors, follow me." Most of the class walked behind Mrs. Ferguson as she started up the grass-covered path. A few kids followed Mrs. Crawford.

"What are you gonna do now, Tom?" asked Jason. Most of the time, Jason, Danny and Tom were good friends. For some reason they felt like hassling him today.

"No way I'm going with you. You guys banged my seat the whole bus ride, even after I asked you to stop. I'm going by myself," said Tom, who zipped up his New York Giants jacket and stomped away from them.

"We didn't mean anything. We promise not to bang your seat on the hike," called Jason.

"I guess you just want to walk with your girlfriend, Sandy Jenkins," teased Danny. Sandy was walking ahead of Tom down the path toward the drydock, straggling behind Mrs. Crawford's group. Sandy had entered Rosendale School only a few weeks ago, and she was having trouble making friends.

Tom spun around. "That does it. You two are dead meat. Keep out of my way so that I don't do permanent injury to your faces." Tom charged toward them, fists clenched. Jason pushed him away.

"No problem. As far as we're concerned, you don't exist. Come on, Danny," said Jason. The two of them hurried to catch up with Mrs. Ferguson.

Tom bent over and picked up a stick that was lying on the path. Mules and horses had once walked along this towpath, pulling the canalboats. He knew that in most of New York State, the canal was filled in and replaced by modern streets and roads. Here though, the canal was still filled with water and looked much the same as it might have 150 years ago, except for the trees. Tom figured that they wouldn't have been growing here long ago because the path had to be clear for the towrope. He walked over to one of the trees and began hitting it angrily with the stick.

"Take it easy," yelled Sandy. "This is a nature preserve."

"Shut up. I'll hit this stupid tree if I want to. You're not my boss." Tom gave an extra hard whack, which sent half of the stick into the canal. He looked back at Sandy, who wore a red buffalo-plaid shirt, blue jeans, and hiking boots. She preferred playing kickball with the boys to joining the girls for jumprope. Her short brown hair added to her boyish appearance. She was very smart, but not well-liked. Tom hadn't paid any attention to her before this moment. She reached down and picked up something. Tom walked over to check it out.

"What's that?" he asked. She was holding a green, gallon-sized bottle. A woven basket was wrapped around it.

"It looks like one of those bottles that hold candles in Italian restaurants," replied Sandy.

"Give it to me."

"Why should I? I found it."

Tom reached over and grabbed for the bottle. Sandy pulled it away at the same time, so that Tom only caught the cork, which popped out of the bottle.

3

A large hand clamped over Tom's mouth and a muscular arm wrapped around his waist. The man lifted Tom over his hard-muscled shoulder. He pounded his fists on the man's back, but the arm around his waist just got tighter. Tom's captor smelled of tobacco and old sweat, as if he hadn't washed for days, maybe even weeks.

"Let me go," Tom screamed. The man ignored him and started walking. Tom heard Sandy's muffled cries behind him. In anger, he sank his teeth into the man's other arm. The man cried out and threw Tom into the air. Tom tensed his body as he was thrown into the canal. Sputtering, he began to tread water. He found that he could just barely stand up, his mouth level with the water surface.

Tom rubbed the water out of his eyes and looked around, trying to make sense out of what had just happened. A team of two mules stood a little to the right of the men on the towpath. A rope ran from the rear mule's harness to an old Erie canalboat. Tom recognized the boat from pictures in a filmstrip that Mrs. Ferguson had shown in school.

Not only did the place look different, it also felt quite different. There was a strange quietness. The constant roar of the airplanes approaching the airport had disappeared. A moment before he had been arguing with Sandy. Now he was in the water and Sandy was draped over the shoulder of a man dressed in old-fashioned clothes.

Another man was standing beside Sandy's captor, holding his arm and cursing Tom. The water felt cold

4

and slimy, so Tom decided to risk swimming back to Sandy and the two waiting men. As soon as he reached the side of the canal, one of the men reached out and hauled Tom out of the water by his shirt collar.

"You bite me again you little devil and I'll throw you into the woods next time. By dang, I'll not have any such behavior while you're working on my boat."

"What do you mean? I'm not working on your boat. I'm on a field trip with my class back there."

"Jeepers creepers, a school kid," said Ned, who was Sandy's captor. "There ain't any time for school during canal season, boy. You're just lyin' runaways."

"We didn't run away," said Tom. "We're here on a field trip with our fourth grade class. Let us go and we'll give you all our money."

Both men roared with laughter. The man holding Sandy was more plump than the other, and just as strong. His round face and blond hair made him appear friendly. He put Sandy down and she shook her short hair.

"You'd better not hurt me. I know karate," she said as she tensed her body and held her hands out in the karate position.

"You ain't gonna get hurt iffn you do as you're told," said the Captain, whose long black beard and hair made him look rather fierce.

"Who are you?" asked Sandy.

"I'm Reuben McWilliams, captain of the 'Annie Lenore.' You call me Captain. This here's Ned, my mate. You two schoolboys will find out soon enough what real work is. Git on board."

No way, thought Tom. If I can get back to the schoolbus, the driver can get help. Then these awful men will leave us alone. His water-soaked boots felt like stones, but he ran for his life up the towpath.

"Git back here you son of a ..." The words were covered by a new sound, the sound of hoofbeats.

Tom looked back and saw Ned riding after him on a mule. His fear became a whip that pushed him faster. The schoolbus should be just ahead, Tom thought. "Just a little farther." He gasped the words to keep up his courage.

"Around this curve and ...oh no!"

Tom stopped running. Ahead of him lay a straight line of towpath, with no sign of his class, the schoolbus, or even the picnic area. Ned caught up to him. He grabbed Tom roughly by the arm, pulled him onto the mule, and laid him over his lap like a sack of potatoes.

"Don't try that again, or I'll thrash you like your Pa never did before," said Ned. "Lay there quiet like and you won't get hurt."

Tom followed Ned's advice and they rode back to the boat. Where's the class? Tom thought.

"We've got a live one here, Captain."

"So I see," said the Captain. "There's a lock up ahead. We'd better stow these hoggees for awhile. I don't want any trouble."

"I'll mind the hayburners. I been doin' it since those other hoggees lit out, I guess another few miles won't kill me." Tom noticed that Ned stooped over and picked up the bottle after he tied up the two mules.

"What's a hoggee?" asked Tom.

6

"Where'd you boys come from, anyways? Everbody knows that hoggees drive the mules that pull the canalboats on the Grand Erie Canal. Now git below, young'uns. We'll see if the Missus has any dry clothes for you," said the Captain.

# CHAPTER TWO

# All Dressed Up

Tom looked over the "Annie Lenore" as he stepped on board. There was a square cabin at each end of the boat. The canalboat had been painted white a long time ago, and had green-shuttered windows spaced evenly on the sides of the cabins. A wooden bridge was lying on the roof of the front cabin. As Tom walked toward the rear of the boat, he passed two large wooden hatches that covered the cargo hold. The rear cabin was similar to the front one. A sooty metal chimney was spreading smoke on the laundry that was hanging between two poles on the roof.

The Captain escorted them down some steps into the rear, or aft, cabin, which served as the living quarters for the crew. The Captain's wife, Grizzy, and their daughter, Rebecca, were cooking lunch. Grizzy and Rebecca were suntanned and wore clean, if a little threadbare, clothes. Rebecca stared at them, and then mumbled a greeting. Her mother, Grizzy, just grunted and turned the fish that she was cooking on the woodstove.

"I brought two new boys to help with the mules, Ma. This here one got a bit wet. Have you any dry clothes for 'im?" asked Captain Reuben.

"Should be one of Rebecca's dresses in the cuddy," replied Grizzy. "He can wear that until his clothes dry."

"Not my other dress," protested Rebecca.

"Don't worry," said Tom. "I'm not gonna wear a dress."

"No sass, boy," said the Captain. "Git in there and do as your told. You go with him." He pointed to a small doorway on the back wall.

"I'm not going to wear a dress and that's final."

"What?" The Captain's eyes blazed and he lunged at Tom, barely missing him. Tom slipped through the blanket that served as a door to the sleeping room. Sandy meekly followed him.

"Now you git some dry clothes on, or I'll beat the daylights out of you," yelled the Captain. "I ain't gonna have no sick hoggees. There's work to be done."

The room was a dingy yellow, like the faded sunflowers along the towpath. It was divided into two parts by another blanket. They identified Rebecca's side by the rag doll lying on her bunk. Tom went to a small trunk and pulled out a red-checked dress.

"Very attractive, Tom. It matches your eyes."

"Shut up. What are we going to do?" asked Tom.

"Beats me. They think I'm a boy," said Sandy.

"Well, I guess I can help you better if they think that we're both boys."

"Help me? What makes you think that I need your help? I've watched you in class. You're always picking on girls. My mom says it's because you're immature. Maybe I'm going to have to help you."

"Me? Immature?" yelled Tom. "Your mom doesn't even know me. Besides, I have friends, which is more than I can say for you."

9

"You pig," Sandy shouted. "I had lots of friends at my old school. Everybody at this school's a bunch of snobs."

"Stop calling me names," warned Tom. "We'll have to stick together if we're ever going to get out of this mess. So how about it? Can you pretend that you're a boy for awhile?"

"I guess so, but you'd better be nicer."

"Okay, I will. Do you really know karate?"

"No," replied Sandy. "I just started the class."

"Too bad, it might have come in handy," said Tom.

"You'd better get that dress on. The Captain seems mean."

"You promise you won't tell the kids at school?"

"Look, Tom. Even if we see the kids again, they'll never believe us," said Sandy.

"Okay, I don't want a beating. Turn around, please. I have to get changed. See, I'm being nice."

Sandy turned and looked into the room on the other side of the blanket. It was the same dirty yellow color, and had a larger bed in the middle and two chests against the wall.

Above the chests was a stained map of New York State, with the route of the Erie Canal traced in red crayon. Below it was a calendar.

"Tom, there's a calendar on this wall."

"So?"

"It says 1829."

"Well," said Tom. "These people look like antiques, maybe they collect them too. Could you help me with this?"

Sandy turned around and laughed when she saw Tom struggling with the dress. "No wonder. You have it on backwards. This cute little ruffle goes in the front."

"Since when do you know about dresses? I've never seen you wear one. You're such a tomboy."

"My mom makes me wear a dress when we go out to a fancy restaurant. I have two at home, but I hate to wear them. I don't look as cute in dresses as you do."

Tom made a face at her. He pulled his hands out of the arms and they both turned it around his waist. He put his arms back into the sleeves and Sandy helped button up the back. "I guess I'm ready. Let's go out and get some answers."

Back in the main part of the cabin, Ned and the Captain were finishing their meal.

"Well, don't you look darlin'," said the Captain. Tom glared at him, but said nothing.

"Listen, sir," said Sandy, "We would like to know what's going on." She searched for a spark of kindness in his eyes, but was met by a cold stare.

"It's simple. You two are a goin' to work with them mules. We caught you stealin' Ned's bottle, so you must be runaways or something. Now you're workin' for me." Ned and the Captain gave their empty plates to Rebecca and started up the steps. "When you've eaten, come up on deck," he called through the doorway.

"Sit." Grizzy motioned to a small table across the cabin from the wood-burning stove. Tom and Sandy sat on the small chairs and watched Rebecca as she served them each a plate of fried fish and potatoes. Then she went to an upright, wooden chest with four doors on the front.  She opened one, pulled out a metal pail, and poured milk into three glasses. The old-fashioned milk pail looked like one that Tom had seen in an antique store that his mother had dragged him to one Saturday. Tom was thirsty and gulped down half a glassful before he realized that it didn't taste like the milk that he drank at home.

"Sandy, taste this stuff.  It's like liquid cheese!"

Sandy took a sip and wrinkled her nose. "It tastes sour.  What is it?"

"Skimmagig, what else?" Rebecca eyed them curiously.

She wasn't sure that she liked these strange kids. They had a curious way of speaking, and their clothes looked as if they had just been bought at a store. Store-boughten clothes were special to Rebecca since all of her clothes were made by her mother.  Seeing their puzzled looks she  added, "Some folks call it buttermilk, but we call it skimmagig here on the Erie."

"Oh, like buttermilk pancakes, I didn't know you could drink it," said Sandy.

"Stop jawin' and eat up.  Captain's got work for you," said Grizzy.  She was a stern woman and only a few inches taller than Rebecca.

Tom ate quietly.  Rebecca was sitting across from him and they stared at each other until she looked away.  She had long dark hair that was carefully brushed, but had not been washed recently.  Her blue-checked dress was similar to the red one that Tom was wearing. Tom finished his meal and handed his glass and plate to Grizzy.

"All right you two. It's time to learn how to earn your keep," said Grizzy. "Go up and help them change those mules."

"I'm not going out there in a dress," said Tom.

"Reuben, git down here," yelled Grizzy.

"I reckon you're gonna get it now," said Rebecca.

The Captain charged down the steps and looked at Grizzy.

"More trouble from that one," she said.

The Captain smacked Tom's head and pushed him up the steps and toward the front of the boat where the mules were kept. Tom kept his balance by catching himself on a large barrel. His eyes watered a little, more from fright than from pain. "Any more trouble from you and I'll tie rocks around you and sink you in the canal," threatened the Captain. "They won't find you 'til spring."

Tom swallowed hard. It was difficult to decide which was worse, drowning or being seen wearing a dress. He chose the dress. Nobody knows me anyway, he thought.

# CHAPTER THREE

# Changing Mules

The front cabin, called the bowstable, was open to the sky, as if someone had sliced it like a square vanilla cake and eaten the middle third. A cover that fit over the opening was lying on the front of the roof. On the Erie Canal, the mules worked in teams, one pair would pull the "Annie Lenore" while the other team rested in the bowstable. The teams were changed every six hours. All four mules returned to the bowstable when the boat stopped for the night. A wooden bridge was stored on the bowstable roof. The Captain and Ned slid it toward Tom and Sandy.

"Take the end of this bridge and pull it in between the boat and the towpath," ordered the Captain.

Tom and Sandy grabbed the end of it and pulled. It was heavy, but slid easily once it began moving. Too easily. They lost their grip and the end crashed into the bank.

"Jeepers creepers, why do I always get fools? Ain't you ever worked on a canalboat before?" stormed the Captain.

"No sir. We never even saw a canalboat before today," said Sandy.

"I knew it. Farmers. You know 'bout drivin' mules, don't you?"

"Where we come from you can't drive until you're sixteen," said Tom. "And there aren't any mules in our neighborhood. Just jackasses." Sandy giggled.

14

"Just my luck. Useless young'uns. Get that bridge up," said the Captain.

"If we're so useless, why don't you let us go?" said Sandy as they jumped onto the bank. They pulled with all their strength, but the bridge only moved about two inches.

"We've got to pull harder, Tom," said Sandy.

"No kidding, I thought that we could use mental telepathy and have it move by itself."

"Telekinesis. Moving objects with your mind is called telekinesis. Don't be nasty."

"Great. We're kidnapped and you give me a vocabulary lesson," scolded Tom. "You always act like the class genius or something. Grab it again. Let's do it. One, two, three."

They strained as hard as they could, but it wasn't enough. The bridge was stuck. Ned jumped down and quickly got the bridge into position.

"It's easier if you put the bridge on the towpath instead of in it," jeered Ned.

"Thanks. We'll remember that," said Sandy. Tom and Sandy looked embarrassed because Ned had made it look so easy.

The Captain appeared from below deck leading a mule. Ned met him at the top of the bridge and took the halter. The Captain placed himself behind the mule and held its tail while the mule walked quietly down the bridge.

"You young'uns hold Jupiter here," said the Captain. Tom clung to the harness fearfully, but the mule showed no interest in running away.

15

The Captain led one of the mules up the bridge and soon reappeared with Mercury, the mule that worked with Jupiter. "Put Comet here into a stall, and watch out, he bites."

Sandy took Comet's halter and led him up the bridge into the bowstable. "Nice, mule," she tried to soothe herself more than the mule. "Don't bite and you'll get some hay, or whatever you eat." The mule seemed to understand and went eagerly into the stall. There was a row of four stalls on one side of the cabin. Opposite the stalls were bales of hay and what appeared to be two straw mattresses. Some buckets and a pitchfork were hanging on the wall. Sandy walked out of the bowstable.

Jupiter and Mercury were hitched in a line, not side by side. Mercury's harness was connected by two ropes to Jupiter's. Behind Jupiter hung a trapeze-like harness to which the towrope was tied. When everything was secure, Ned mounted Jupiter and the mules walked forward, tightening the slack of the 100 foot towrope.

"Git below, young'uns and make yourself scarce. Stay put until I give the word. No foolishness," ordered the Captain.

Tom and Sandy jumped onto the deck and headed for the cabin. Grizzy and Rebecca had just finished putting away the dishes from dinner, the noon meal. There was no sink, just a galvanized metal tub filled with greasy water sitting on the table.

"We're supposed to hide in here while we go through a lock," said Tom.

16

Grizzy motioned to the chairs by the table. As they sat down, she picked up the tub and went up on deck. Rebecca followed, carrying a wicker washbasket containing Tom's wet clothes. As soon as they were gone, Tom and Sandy moved the chairs and each looked out one of the two small windows on the towpath side. They saw Grizzy dump the dishwater into the canal.

"They don't care much about pollution," grumbled Sandy.

"Sandy, there weren't any picnic tables up ahead."

"I noticed. You were pretty stupid to run away."

"I had to try something. I didn't see you helping any," said Tom.

"I thought you were going to save me," said Sandy. "I'm scared, Tom. We don't have any idea how we got here. We need to do some planning, not running."

"Maybe we'll find a time machine or a mad scientist," said Tom.

"Stop joking. I'll bet you're just as scared as I am."

"Okay, I'm scared, too," said Tom. "I guess we'll have to run and stop the next car that we see on the road."

"You mean that road?" Sandy pointed to the right. The smooth, paved road was now a narrow dirt one, with ruts made by wagons, not cars.

"How can a whole road disappear?" said Tom. "What is going on?"

"Tom. What if we really are in 1829?"

"That's impossible."

"We'd better try to talk to that girl," said Sandy. "Maybe she will help us."

17

# CHAPTER FOUR

# Rebecca Gets Her Wish

"Ma, I don't like them new hoggees. They act funny," said Rebecca. She was hanging Tom's wet clothes on a rope that stretched across the roof of the rear cabindeck and served as the family clothesline. The morning laundry was dry, and her mother was taking it down.

"Now Rebecca, don't be so quick to judge. The good Lord makes all kinds. Your Pa needs help with the mules since them other boys ran off yesterday," replied Grizzy.

"I guess so, but look at this coat. There's letters on the back. Can you read 'em?" Rebecca fingered Tom's football jacket.

"I ain't had much schoolin', but I know that these here spell New York. I don't know what G-I-A-N-T-S spells. Imagine puttin' words on good clothing. These clothes look store-boughten to me. Maybe we've got some rich young'uns. You finish up this wash and take it below. I have to talk to your Pa." Grizzy stepped off the rear cabin roof and went a few steps to the tiller where the Captain was standing.

After she had finished hanging Tom's clothes on the clothesline, Rebecca neatly folded the dry clothes and stacked them inside the wicker basket. She picked up the laundry and carried it back down to the cabin. The bulky basket bumped against her legs as she walked down the steps. She glanced at Tom and Sandy, and

18

then took her burden into the sleeping compartment, which canallers called a cuddy. She began to sort the laundry, making piles for her mother, father, Ned and herself.

"Your duds'll dry quick." She spoke through the blanket-door. "Then you can get out of my dress."

"Thanks," said Tom.

"Your duds don't look like the kind we have on the canal. Where'd you get 'em?"

"I don't know. Probably at the mall."

"Mall? What's that?"

"You know, a place to go shopping," said Sandy.

"I ain't never heard of a mall. There's canal stores for shopping, but I ain't heard of any of 'em called Mall."

"It's in Niskayuna."

"The only store around here is in Rexford Flats. There ain't any stores in Niskayuna that I know of, just some farmers. Is your Pa a farmer?"

"No, he isn't," said Sandy. "He works for General Electric."

"Never heard of him. Only generals I heard of are President Jackson and General Washington."

"No, it's not a person, it's a company. They make dishwashers and light bulbs and TV sets."

Rebecca looked very confused. "Are you making this up?"

"It's not me that's making things up. You just said that the president's name was Jackson," said Tom.

"Maybe we'd better change the subject. Could I ask you some questions?" said Sandy in a soothing voice.

"I guess," replied Rebecca.

"What year is it?" asked Sandy.

"What year? It's 1829."

"1829?" said Tom. "Are you sure?"

"Sure I am. Fancy not knowin' the year."

"How old are you?" asked Sandy.

"Ten," answered Rebecca.

"That means you were born in 1819," said Tom.

"How'd you figure that out?"

"You subtract 10 from 1829. How else?" he said.

Rebecca's eyes widened. "You been to school?"

"Of course," said Sandy. "In fact, we're supposed to be in school now, except that your father kidnapped us."

"How come you don't know what year it is iffn you been to school? Can you read?" asked Rebecca.

"Sure, can't you?" said Sandy.

"What's it say on your jacket?"

"New York Giants," replied Tom.

"There ain't no giants in New York. They're just make believe. You two are strange. You don't know the year. You believe in giants, and malls, and I don't know what all."

"Let's not talk about it now," said Tom. He wondered whether Rebecca was telling the truth about it being 1829. That was the same year that was on the calendar in the cuddy. Could he trust Rebecca enough to tell her that it was really 150 years later? Would she help them escape, or would she tell her parents? I'd better get to know her better before I trust her, he thought.

"Would you help me with my readin' ?" asked Rebecca.

"We'll think about it," replied Sandy.

Rebecca's face brightened as she thought about learning to read at last. She longed for the time when those jumbles of letters would make sense. Living on the canal, Rebecca only had a chance to go to school in the winter. Her parents had let her go for the winter term last year after the canal closed for the season, but she hadn't learned much. They had promised that she could go again this winter.

"Just think. I'll be able to read," said Rebecca.

"Reading's not that big a deal," said Tom. "Mostly you do workbook pages and answer questions that the teacher asks you."

"I think it's excitin.' Wait until Ma and Pa hear about this." She ran happily up on deck to tell her parents the news.

Tom looked anxiously at Sandy. "She said it's 1829. Just like the calendar said." He whispered to be sure that the Captain, who was standing right outside the cabin door steering the boat with the tiller, didn't overhear him. "Do you know what that means?"

"Uh-huh. We guessed right," said Sandy. "We really have travelled back in time."

"But that only happens in books and movies." said Tom.

"Uh-huh."

"Doesn't that upset you? Say something besides uh-huh."

"Look, I don't understand any of this. I'm scared, I want to go home, and if I don't stay calm, I'll cry." Sandy felt her eyes fill with tears.

"That's okay. You can cry. I won't laugh or anything." Tom was not good at comforting others. Sometimes when his little sister hurt herself he would run away instead of giving her a hug. He didn't feel good about it, but he couldn't help himself. Besides, he wasn't about to hug Sandy. "So, do you think it really is 1829?" he asked, trying to keep the conversation going.

"She didn't know about TV, or malls, or football," replied Sandy.

"How are we ever going to get home?"

"I don't know. I guess we have to figure out how we got here," said Sandy.

"Did you see any space ships?" asked Tom.

"Of course not."

"Little green men?"

"Be serious. I was walking down the path by myself. You were there," said Sandy.

"Why didn't you make some friends?" Tom regretted his remark as soon as it slipped out. "I mean, why were you walking behind Mrs. Crawford's group?"

"Those stuck-up girls won't be with me. I wish I hadn't moved."

"Yeah, I know." Tom had lived in the same house all of his life, but some of his friends had told him how hard it was to move into a new neighborhood. He couldn't think of the right thing to say, so he looked out at the men who were busy getting the "Annie Lenore" through the lock. The towrope had been untied from the mules' harness, and a few men were towing the boat through the lock gate. When it was in position, the locktenders closed the gates. Tom felt the boat move slightly as the water began to pour into the lock. He knew from his studies at school that the water came in from the bottom, raising the boat to the upper level of the canal. As he stared out the small window, the gray rock sides of the lock seemed to sink as the boat was raised. I hope that this is on the Social Studies test, he thought. I'm going to be an expert on locks before this is over. Finally, the water had raised the "Annie Lenore" to the top of the lock. The rope was tied to the mules again, and Ned led them out of the upper gate and westward up the towpath.

"Git ready, you two," shouted the Captain. "As soon as we get out of sight, you're gonna become canallers."

# CHAPTER FIVE

# Hoggee Lessons

"Now all you have to do is walk with these mules and keep them moving. They'll want to eat grass, or walk across some farmer's field. Don't let 'em," said Ned. The "Annie Lenore" had stopped long enough for Tom and Sandy to jump onto the towpath and meet Ned and the mules. "I'll walk along with you for a while and show you the ropes."

"We know what ropes are," Tom wisecracked.

"No sass, young'un." Ned whacked Tom across the head. Tom stumbled and fell onto the towpath, narrowly avoiding a pile of fresh manure.

Sandy turned around to see if Tom was all right, but kept walking in fear that Ned would hit her also. Tom brushed himself off and caught up.

Tom walked along quietly with the others. He found it curious that the weather was about the same as it had been when he had left for school this morning. It was a crisp, blue-sky day. The sun was bright and still had enough strength to warm him. It sparkled on the water, making the canal look like a sheet of aluminum foil. I guess they don't have aluminum foil in 1829, Tom thought. Will I ever see my real life things again? He scratched his side. He had changed back into his own clothes, but they were still damp and made him itch.

"Ned," Tom broke the silence. "What did the Captain mean when he said that we stole your bottle?"

"The one you was holding when we invited you to work for us?"

"Yeah. I know it's funny, but I can't seem to remember what happened. Would you tell us?"

"Hmmmm." Ned pulled up his pants, which had a habit of slipping under his ample waist. "Back toward Crescent I found an empty bottle lyin' on the towpath. It still had the cork in it. I figured it might be good for something, so I carried it along. I set it down when we were gettin' ready to change the mules. The Captain and I started to unhitch them and there was you two fightin' over the bottle. You must have been fightin' hard not to have heard us."

"Did you see us before we had the bottle?" asked Tom.

"No. Were you in the woods or somethin'?"

"I don't remember. It must be amnesia," said Tom.

"I ain't had that yet. Is it catching?"

"No. It's when you get bumped on the head and lose your memory for a while," said Sandy. "Another thing that we can't remember is what year it is. Can you tell us the date?"

"Yes, it's November in 1829," answered Ned.

Sandy's eyes filled with tears as she looked at Tom. She had begun to believe that they really were trapped in 1829. "Can these two mules pull that heavy boat?"

"Sure, once she gets movin', she sort of glides by herself slick as you please."

A shrill blast from the Captain's horn interrupted their conversation. "Packet comin," the Captain yelled.

"I don't suppose you two know what to do," said Ned.

Tom and Sandy shook their heads. Tom looked back at the packet boat. He remembered reading in his history book that these boats carried passengers and went faster than freighters. Captain Rueben steered the "Annie Lenore" into the center of the canal. Ned stopped the mules and let the towrope go slack so that the packet could pass right over it. The packet was an impressive sight with three matching black horses pulling it. The hoggee was dressed in a uniform and rode on the back of the rear horse. He looked at Tom and Sandy in disgust, acting like he was superior to other hoggees. Passengers were sitting on the top deck, smoking or reading newspapers. They looked comfortable and unconcerned about the other traffic on the canal. The steersman waved to Ned as the boat hurried by.

"Full freightings to ya," he yelled. This was the customary greeting among canallers.

Ned waved back. "Now you know what to do if a boat passes you in the same direction. Just make sure them mules don't get tangled," said Ned. "Tom, you take the mules now, then we'll give Sandy a turn. Tomorrow we start the regular six hour shifts."

Watching Ned and Sandy head back to the boat, Tom felt a twinge of panic. Could he control these mules? At home he even had trouble making his dog listen.

"Git 'em movin'," yelled Ned as he stepped on board.

Tom yelled "giddap" and jerked the reins. He imagined he was John Wayne, leading homesteaders across the prairie. "Hee yaaa," he called again. The mules snorted and began moving forward, taking up the slack in the towrope. Not exactly a legendary start, but they didn't run away. They seemed to know the pace, so Tom just followed them. As he walked, his panic lessoned and his mind wandered. I wonder if the class is frantically looking for me, he thought. Did anyone call Mom or Dad? The police? The FBI? I'm beginning to feel homesick again.

He tried singing to lift his spirits. "99 bottles of beer on the wall, 99 bottles of beer. Take one down, pass it around, 98 bottles of beer on the wall." But singing just made him feel sadder, reminding him of his school friends.

A few years ago, he had gone to summer camp for the first time. He remembered sitting in front of his tent, crying because he missed his parents. He begged his counselor, Mike, to let him call home. Mike told him that it was normal to be homesick and that the best cure was to keep busy. Tom went down to the stables and took horseback riding lessons. He was so worried about falling off the horse that he never thought of home. After that, he spent a lot of time riding and his homesickness disappeared. He'd never ridden a mule, though.

Thinking about riding gave him an idea. If the packet hoggee could ride, so could he. He stopped the mule team and tried to climb on the back of Jupiter. The mule's back was a little high, but he managed to boost himself up by grabbing the mule's neck and swinging his legs up. He gave a kick with his heels and the mules resumed their pace before the "Annie Lenore" stopped coasting.

Tom felt better on top of the mule. As he rode, he looked around and tried to notice the differences in the landscape. The Mohawk River was a lot shallower than he remembered. A chilly gust of wind reminded him that he wasn't really dressed for cold weather. The Rexford Aqueduct came into view as they rounded a bend in the river. On Tom's right were cliffs that he'd seen many times on his way to Saratoga. Soon he was riding across the aqueduct, a bridge that carried the canal across the river. The aqueduct was so quiet, unlike the busy bridge that was used in modern times. There was a large hotel on the northern bank that must have been torn down to make way for the modern road, he thought. He felt dizzy when he looked over the side of the aqueduct. The Mohawk River looked like it was just waiting to swallow him up. He tried to look ahead, not down.

After what seemed to be no time at all, he heard the familiar trumpet blast from the Captain. Sandy had jumped off the boat and was coming toward him. Tom stopped the mules and dismounted.

"We're almost in Schenectady and I'm supposed to take over," said Sandy.

"Why? It seems like I just got started."

"I don't know," said Sandy. "The Captain said to switch. Where'd you learn how to ride?"

"Summer camp. It's better riding than walking. Here, I'll give you a boost up."

"I don't know. I've only ridden those pony rides where they hold onto the reins and lead you around. Are they gentle?"

"It's easy. They run on automatic pilot. You just have to keep them on the towpath."

"Are you actually being nice to me, or do you want me to fall and break my neck?"

"I don't care what you do," said Tom as he turned and started back to the boat.

"Okay, I'll try it," shouted Sandy.

"Good for you."

Sandy tried to climb up onto the mule's slippery back. She was a few inches shorter than Tom, and after several failed attempts, she called for help.

"Come on Tom," she pleaded. "Give me a boost."

"I thought you didn't need any help from me."

"We're going to have to help each other if we're going to get out of here. I just meant that it wasn't always going to be you helping me. Please?"

"Okay." Tom grabbed her foot and boosted her up.

Once settled, she said, "I brushed and fed the other mule team, so you can relax."

"Great. I'll take a nap. I feel like today has been about a month long. Good luck." Tom slapped the back of the mule to get it moving, then walked back to the boat.

# CHAPTER SIX

# Making Peace

Back on board the "Annie Lenore," Tom sat atop the bowstable and looked for familiar sights in the city. At home, he went into Schenectady several times a week to visit the library or to shop with his mom. A busy dock, where many boats were being loaded or unloaded, was in about the same place where his mom usually parked the car. The spires of the Episcopal and Presbyterian churches seemed to grow above the city like giant trees. In modern times they were hidden by taller buildings. Men worked or relaxed in front of the many stores and warehouses along the canal. One store had a sign that said "General Merchandise" and had a man's coat draped over a mannequin in the window. Tom wished that he had his camera. The museum would love to see those pictures, he thought.

Sandy looked lost among the many strong workers, who took no notice of her. Her hair was cut in about the same style as theirs and they never suspected that she was a girl. Tom thought that it would be fun to tell the people about the future, but he decided that he'd better not. He had read somewhere that time travellers were not supposed to interfere in the lives of the people that they visit. They wouldn't believe him anyway.

"Whatchadoin'?" asked Rebecca as she climbed up on the cabin roof.

"Just watching the city. Those workers sure look busy," replied Tom.

"Ever been to Schenectady afore?"

"Yeah, my dad works here."

"In that 'General' place that you were tellin' me about?" asked Rebecca.

"Yes. It's around here somewhere. I miss my mom and dad."

"Then you shouldn't have run away."

"I'm tired of explaining this," yelled Tom as he turned to face her. "Your dad and Ned kidnapped us. We were on a school trip. Why can't you ignorant people get that through your heads."

"No need to call me names just because you can read." Rebecca stood up to leave.

"Wait. I'm sorry. Please stay. I like having someone to talk to, then I don't feel so lonely. Tell me about canal life. What time do you wake up?"

"Oh, we don't much follow clocks," said Rebecca as she sat back down again. She kept about four feet between them, though. "Pa wakes us up about daybreak and we stop when it gets too dark to travel."

"Don't the boats travel at night?"

"Some do. Packetboats mostly. Pa says it's kind of dangerous at night what with robbers and drunks."

"What do the robbers do?" asked Tom.

"They sneak about, whacking people over the heads. Then they take their money and throw them into the canal."

"Don't they get caught?"

"Not much. A lot of times the bodies aren't found until they drain the canal before winter. I gotta git, now. Ma's gonna need help fetchin' supper."

After they had passed through Schenectady, Tom asked the Captain where he could take a nap. The Captain pointed to the bowstable and said, "In there."

"With the mules?" Tom asked. The Captain grunted and looked away. "Aye, aye sir." Tom headed back to the bow of the boat. The other team was contentedly munching their feed, and did not pay much attention to Tom as he entered the bowstable. He went over to a pile of straw and fluffed it up to make a bed. The ends of strawstalks poked him in the back when he lay down. He had to keep reaching under himself and rearranging them. The autumn-fresh smell of the straw was pleasant. His mind and body sank comfortably into the soft straw, and soon he was asleep.

Several hours later, Tom and Sandy were back in the bowstable preparing for their first night in a canalboat.

"I guess we don't have to worry about getting changed in front of each other since we haven't any other clothes," said Tom as they were each fluffing up their straw beds.

"That's true. I can't see much with that lantern , anyway. Can you make it brighter?"

"Sure, we have one of these at home. You just turn this knob to raise the wick," said Tom. The flame in the lantern got brighter as Tom turned the wick higher. Thick smoke poured from the top of the chimney, blackening the glass and making it darker again."

"Now you've done it," said Sandy. "That smoke made the light dimmer, and it stinks. What do they burn in that lantern?"

"I don't know. I'm new here, all right? Give me a break," snarled Tom.

"Okay, but turn it back down. Where do we go to the bathroom?"

"That bucket over in the corner. When you're done dump it into the canal."

"You're kidding."

"I'm serious."

"That's gross, but I'm desperate. Only I'm moving it behind the stable."

"Go ahead." Tom took off his shoes and massaged his feet. He was glad that he'd decided to wear his hiking boots on the field trip instead of his sneakers. People stared at his clothes enough. His sneakers would have stuck out like white paws on a black cat. He had finished kneading the second foot when Sandy returned.

"Remind me not to go swimming in the canal," she said.

"It's not too pleasant," Tom agreed, remembering when he was thrown into the canal.

"Right. Okay, so how are we going to get home?"

"Did you talk to Ned while you were walking with him in Schenectady?" asked Tom.

"Yes. He insists that nothing weird happened. We were just holding the bottle," said Sandy. "Maybe there's a genie inside."

"Come on, Sandy. There are no such things as genies."

"Okay, then how did we get here?"

"I don't know. Maybe there's a magic potion in the bottle," said Tom.

"Of course. A magic potion. Excuse me for being so dumb. Magic potions are so much more realistic than genies. I'm so foolish for not thinking of that."

"All right, Sandy, stop it. Did you find out anything more from Ned?"

"He said that he's saving the bottle for his girlfriend, who is a cook on a boat called 'The Genesee Gent'." said Sandy. "He's going to give it to her when they meet at the next lock. It seems that they have big crowds at locks."

"Do you really think that the bottle is the key to getting us back home?"

"It seems like a good place to start, Tom. I don't remember anything else."

"I guess then we've got to get that bottle before he gives it away. I have the first shift tomorrow. Can you sneak into his cabin and get it?"

"I'll try," said Sandy. "I'll get it right before we change mules. Then I'll hop onto the towpath. Now that we have a plan, I'm going to sleep. Good night."

"Good night, Sandy. I guess we're going to have to get along on this adventure."

"I agree, but you make me so mad when you act like you know it all."

"Okay, I'll try to be nicer if you will."

"Okay, we'll both try harder. Maybe we can get the bottle tomorrow and be home by tomorrow night."

"I hope so," replied Tom as he rolled over and closed his eyes.

# CHAPTER SEVEN

# Grave Robbers

Tom was awakened by the sound of Mercury's tail knocking over the empty water bucket. The cabin's darkness felt like the inside of a cave and Tom needed to get out for awhile and breathe fresh air. He couldn't see Sandy, but could hear her slow, sleepy breathing. He put on his boots and stood up. By now, he knew the layout of the cabin well enough so that he could find his way in the dark.

"The stall is across the cabin, so I have to walk left to get around it." Tom whispered these facts to himself, partly to remember the way to the cabin door, but mostly to keep up his courage. "Okay, here's the wall, so I keep my left hand on it to get to the door. Slowly. Quietly. Don't wake up anybody." He felt his way using the wall as a guide. He got to the door and reached for a light switch on the wall out of habit. "No, dummy, electric lights haven't been invented yet." The cabin door groaned as he began sliding it open, but once it got going it was pretty quiet. "No sense opening this door any more than I have to." The full moon and bright stars lit the way as he squeezed through the small opening that he had made.

Tom jumped from the canalboat to the towpath and took a few deep breaths. Ah, he thought to himself, this is more like it. It was a beautiful night, much too wonderful to spend cooped up with the mules. The Big Dipper hung in the sky above the line of canalboats that

35

were tied up for the night.  Looking down the towpath, he thought he saw the outline of a wagon heading his way.

"That can't be.  It must be pretty late."  He remembered his wristwatch that was lying on his dresser at home.  The wagon seemed to be getting closer, so he crossed the towpath and hid behind a tree.

The wagon moved quietly toward where he was hiding.  It was small, about the size of a buggy.  One horse was hitched to it. It's hooves were covered with cloth or leather so that the horse walked almost silently.  The wagon's moving parts had been heavily greased and barely made a sound.  The driver was hunched over, whispering to a tall man who was walking on the canalside.  The tall man was looking closely at each canalboat as they went by.

"Whoa."  The man in the driver's seat stopped the wagon about twenty feet beyond Tom.  The other man leaned against the wagon and looked into the woods. It's lucky they didn't stop in front of me, thought Tom. He caught a glimpse of a lumpy sack lying on the wagonbed and smelled the odor of newly dug ground.

"What did yer say the name o' this here boat was?" asked the driver, whose long grey hair stuck out of his hat like fringe.

"The Resurrection," replied the man on the ground. Tom strained to see what he looked like, but could only tell that he was tall.  "Do you see it?"

"I see lotsa boats, but I cain't make out any names. Ya knows I cain't read."

"Well, I can read some, but it's hard to make out these long words. There was supposed to be a signal. I'll walk ahead and take a look. Maybe the captain forgot to hang out the two signal lights."

"I'm comin' too. This sneakin' about gives me the creeps." The driver got down from the wagon and both men walked up the towpath looking at the names of the boats.

Tom peeked out from his hiding place. I wonder what's in that wagon, he thought. It was in a dirty sack. Tom decided to risk a closer look and carefully approached the back of the wagon. The earthy smell reminded him of a sack of potatoes. I wonder what it is, Tom thought. I'll just take a peek and go back to the tree. They'll never see me.

There was enough light for Tom to find the string that closed the bag. He untied it and reached in, releasing another odor that was more foul. His hand found something that was too big for a potato. Zucchini, thought Tom. He pulled at it, but it was attached to something else. It felt soft and limp, sort of like meat. At the top, there were some things that wiggled when he moved them. Tom lifted the bag back to take a look. It was a human foot!

"AAAAAAAH!" Tom let out a gasp of shock, quickly released the foot, and ran back to his hiding place. Safely behind the tree, he stood motionless, trying to understand what was happening. The sack contained a body! He took some deep breaths, trying to calm himself. Shivers ran up and down his body, and his arm broke out in goosebumps. He stared at his hand.

Yuck, he thought, I actually touched a dead person! He wiped his hands on the newly fallen leaves, trying to remove an imagined stain.

He stood up, calmer now, and tightly gripped the tree trunk. Swallowing his fear, he peeked around the trunk. The white foot seemed to glow amongst the dark shapes and shadows of the wagon bed.

Uh oh, he thought, the foot is sticking out. What if they notice. They'll come looking for me! He decided to go back to the wagon and cover up the foot. Slowly, he loosened his grip on the tree. Come on legs, move. He inched forward, concentrating on the foot, pretending that it wasn't evil or scary. Just somebody's foot. It got easier as he approached the wagon.

Soon, he was staring at the foot from the end of the wagon. Tentatively, he reached for the cloth. He glimpsed a movement on his right. He looked up in time to see a hand reach around and grab him. Instantly another hand clamped over his mouth.

"Don't make a sound." It was the taller man who had come back to the wagon. "What are you doing around here?" He removed his hand from Tom's mouth.

"Ah. I ah. I work on that boat."

"In the middle of the night?"

Tom's wits began to recover. "Actually, I couldn't sleep so I came out for a walk. Lovely night isn't it?"

"Look at what we got here," said the driver as he arrived back at the wagon. "Could he be 'nother specimen?"

"Shut up," said the taller man. "Tell me more, young'un."

"Well, my friend and I were kidnapped by Captain Reuben and he made us work. We have to sleep with the mules. I woke up and the cabin was stuffy. I saw your wagon and hid in those woods. I'm sorry that the person in the wagon died."

"Jeepers creepers, ain't he a smart one?" said the driver. "Can you read?"

"Of course I can. Can't you?"

"Shut up kid. We don't like kids, 'specially ones that nose around our business," the tall man looked menacing again. "What are we going to do with you?"

"Let's throw 'im into the canal," said the driver. "Then we can sell 'im."

"I told you to shut up. If you can read, kid, what's the name of that boat?"

"The 'George Washington'."

"Hmm. Suppose you come along with us. We're looking for a boat called 'The Resurrection.' You can help us find it."

Tom didn't have much choice so he agreed to help them. The driver climbed up into the wagon seat and followed Tom and the tall man as they searched for the boat. Tom walked close to the canal so that he could read the boat names in the moonlight.

"Stop." The two men and Tom turned around and saw Ned stepping onto the towpath, a shotgun aimed at them. "Let that boy alone. He's no concern of yours."

"Says who?" the driver said as he reached into the wagonbed.

39

"Don't try it mister. I'm the mate on the 'Annie Lenore' and that boy is our hoggee. Let him go and there won't be any trouble."

"We caught him snooping around our wagon. We got some secret cargo," said the tall man.

"I can see that. I have no quarrel with graverobbers. I'll see to it that the boy doesn't say anything. Now git."

"We could use 'im. We're tyin' to find 'The Resurrection' and we cain't make out all these dang long words," said the driver.

"That boat is up the line a bit. Captain Stark's wife hung up a lot of laundry tonight. You can't miss it."

Deciding that the conversation had ended, the tall man pulled the sack back over the body in the wagonbed. He stepped to the front of the horse and began walking ahead. The driver flicked the reins on the horse and moved on also. Ned and Tom silently watched them.

Tom breathed a sigh of relief. "Thanks Ned."

"Let's get on board. Why were you galavanting around tonight?"

"I woke up and thought I'd get some air. I wasn't trying to run away."

"Mebbe not, but stay away from graverobbers."

"What do they do?" asked Tom as they walked back to the "Annie Lenore."

"They dig up newly buried bodies and sell 'em to doctor schools. Helps folks learn doctorin'. Makes me sick."

"Me too." Tom shivered at the thought. "by the way, how come the lanterns stink? We almost died from the smell in the bowstable, and yours stinks, too."

"We burn grease in 'em," Ned explained. w"henever Mrs. McWilliams has leftover fryin' grease, she saves it for the lanterns."

"Oh," said Tom. They stepped on board the canalboat. "Well, goodnight."

"Night," said Ned as they both headed back to their bunks.

THE CANAL BOY

# CHAPTER EIGHT

# A SECRET IS DISCOVERED

The next morning, Sandy was sitting on top of the bowstable watching Tom on the towpath. The Captain had given them an old straw hat to shade their heads when they were working on the towpath. They only had one, so they shared it. Tom looked funny riding on Jupiter with his blue NY Giants jacket and that old hat. This morning he had told her about his encounter with the graverobbers and she had been horrified. It strengthened her resolve to get back home.

"I will get back," she said aloud.

"Get back where?" Rebecca came up from below deck and sat down beside her. She was wearing the same dress that she wore yesterday and was twirling her stringy black hair.

"Back home," said Sandy. "I miss my parents and my friends."

"A brave boy shouldn't be whining for his parents," said Rebecca.

"I'm not a boy!" The words burst out before she could stop them. "I mean I'm not a boy who is all that brave." She looked toward the towpath, avoiding Rebecca's eyes.

Rebecca looked at Sandy suspiciously, then said, "Tell me about what your school's like."

"There's not much to tell," said Sandy. "Besides, I think that your school is too different from mine for you to understand." She wanted this conversation to end before she blabbed out more. She looked down at her dirty arm. "Is there somewhere I could take a bath?"

"A bath? What do you want to do that for?" asked Rebecca. "It ain't even Saturday."

"So what?"

"Saturday's bath day."

"I take a bath every day."

"You're the queerest boy I ever knowed. But if you're determined, there's a washtub in the cabin. Heat the water on the stove and go to it. I'm gonna sit here and enjoy the sunshine."

"Too much sun causes cancer."

"What?"

"Never mind. See you later."

Sandy walked to the cabin in the rear of the "Annie Lenore," relieved that she didn't have to talk to Rebecca any more. In the kitchen, she found the captain's wife, who had just finished cleaning up the breakfast dishes. There was nothing on the stove, so Rebecca asked if she could heat up some water for a bath.

"Ain't Saturday," said Grizzy.

"I know, but I want a bath anyway."

"Suit yourself. The tub's over there. You can put it in Rebecca's room. I'm goin' up to see if there's any fish on the trawl line."

Sandy remembered reading in her Social Studies book that canalboat families dragged a fishing line, called a trawl line, behind their boats. The fish that they caught provided free meals. Food that they couldn't catch was bought in the many stores that were found along the canal, or from boats that sold fresh vegetables and meat.

She found the grey metal washtub leaning against the corner by the stove. Her grandma had one just like it in her basement and had told Sandy that it was used for washing clothes before washing machines were invented. It was too small for her to sit in, but large enough to squat and sponge the water over her body. She lifted the heavy iron kettle onto the stove and went up the steps to get water. There was a bucket on the deck with a rope attached to the handle. Some potato peelings floated by, reminding her that the canal was used as a sewer, but she threw the bucket into the water anyway. The rope dug into her hands when she pulled the bucket up. She peered into the bucket, making sure there was no garbage in the water. Satisfied that the water was clean, she grasped the handle with both hands and headed for the cabin. She had to shuffle with the bucket between her legs to keep the water from spilling, but about half of it spilled anyway. At last she reached the stove and emptied the water into the kettle. After another trip to the canal, the kettle was full. While the water was heating, she took the tub into Rebecca's room. She found a towel and washcloth in the trunk. Laying it next to the tub, she went to get the water and some soap.

Back at the tub, she undressed quickly. There wasn't enough water to take a real bath, so she lathered herself with her hands and washcloth. Mom would call this a sponge bath, she thought. The warm water felt good as it trickled down her body. She began to relax a little as she rinsed herself.

"So, you're a girl after all," said Rebecca peeking her head through the curtain. Sandy gave a shriek and grabbed the towel to cover herself. "I ain't never seen a boy naked, but I reckon I know what a girl looks like."

"Please don't tell," pleaded Sandy, drying herself.

"I won't, for now. Just make sure you keep your promise about teachin' me readin'."

"I promise. Now let me get dressed."

"It's my room, I can be here iffn I want. I'll just sit on the bed and wait for you to tell me why a girl would be pretendin' to be a hoggee."

"Oh, why not," said Sandy. "You won't believe it anyway." While she got dressed, she told Rebecca everything that had happened since she and Tom had arrived at the canal for a field trip. Rebecca stared in amazement, but didn't interrupt.

"Will you help us?" pleaded Sandy when she had finished her story.

Rebecca scratched her head in thought. "That's an unbelievable yarn all right. Could be true. My ma always says that the world is full of mysterious things. On the other hand, you might be fibbin'. I reckon I'll help you iffn you teach me to read."

"Okay, we'll start lessons tonight. You promise not to tell anyone that I'm a girl?"

"Yeah, it'll be our secret," replied Rebecca. "I love secrets."

"The first thing we need to do is sneak into Ned's cabin and get that bottle. Let's go before your ma gets back."

"Ned and I get along pretty good," said Rebecca, "but Pa'd whup me good if he found out I went into Ned's cabin. Maybe I can talk to him and find out where it is."

"You promised to help me."

"I will, it's just that I'm not allowed in Ned's cabin. Besides, iffn I help you now, you'll be gone before our readin' lesson."

This kid's smarter than she looks, thought Sandy. I'd better be a good teacher or she'll stall forever.

A blast from the captain's horn interrupted their conversation. "Lock ahead. Everybody look lively," shouted the Captain.

"Don't forget your promise," warned Sandy.

"I won't," replied Rebecca. Although she intended to keep Sandy's secret, she wasn't sure that she was going to help get the bottle. Her parents had forbidden her to disturb Ned's things and she knew that she would be in big trouble if she got caught. She didn't think that it would be worth the risk for such an unbelievable story.

Out on the towpath, Tom had stopped the mules and waited for the Captain to steer behind a long line of boats waiting to go through the lock. There were many people on the towpath stretching their legs, and talking in small groups. There would be a long wait before the "Annie Lenore" could go through the lock.

"Do ya want me to improve our position in line, Captain?" asked Ned. When she and Rebecca came up on deck, Sandy saw the two men standing by the tiller, which was the rudder used to steer the boat. Ned was pounding his right fist into his left palm.

"Naw, I think I'll get Sprinter and see iffn we can make some money," said the Captain. "Go help the youngun tie up them mules." He disappeared into the aft cabin. Ned jumped onto the towpath and walked toward Tom.

"What did Ned mean when he said that he was going to 'improve our position'?" asked Sandy.

"Ned's a big one, I reckon. Sometimes he goes up the line at locks and finds a boat with a smaller mate. Iffn Ned whups him, we can take their place in line."

"They have fights just to move up ahead in line? Sometimes in school when kids budge, the other kids try to keep them out of line, but I didn't think that grownups did it. Why?"

"Another explaining to do," sighed Rebecca. "You must be from the future. You don't know nothin. Listen careful. Pa signs a paper that says that he'll deliver this load of nails to a man in Buffalo by a certain day. Iffn Pa's late, he gets less money. Iffn Pa's early, the man has to give him a bonus for bein' so fast. Ned can save some time iffn he fights us a better place in line. See?"

"Yes," said Sandy. She decided not to ask who Sprinter was or how he was going to make money.

47

# CHAPTER NINE

# THE CATERPILLAR RACE

"Come on, young'uns. We're gonna see if old Sprinter can earn us some money," said the Captain as he came up from the kitchen. He was carrying an old tobacco can. He's not as mean as he seemed at first, thought Sandy. Maybe he was just trying to make us behave. She and Rebecca followed him up the towpath to where Tom and Ned were waiting.

"What's going on?" asked Tom.

"Caterpillar race. You might as well come along iffn you can stay out of trouble," said the Captain. "Ned, you stay here and hold our place in line."

"Put a dollar on Sprinter for me, Captain," said Ned.

"Caterpillar race?" asked Tom again.

"Pa is gonna find someone who has a caterpillar to race against Sprinter," said Rebecca. "Sprinter's the fastest on the canal. People bet money when we race. Since we always win, we'll get some of it. Sprinter ain't lost yet, has he Pa?"

"Nope. But there's always a first time. It's gettin' late in the season. Not as fast as he used to be. I reckon he'll be a cocoon before long."

As they walked up the line of boats, the Captain stopped and chatted with many people. It seemed that he was well known by the canallers.

"Still got that caterpillar, Sol?" asked the Captain.

"Naw, I let him go so that he could spin his cocoon afore winter. He got beat too many times anyways. How's the missus?" Sol was leaning against a barrel, smoking his pipe.

"Fine and dandy," replied the Captain.

"Those two new hoggees you got there? I don't recollect seeing them before."

"Yup. I recruited them yesterday. They're greenhorns, but they're learnin'."

"Mighty unusual clothes, wouldn't you say?" asked Sol.

"Store-boughten, I guess. They ain't been on the canal before. I didn't ask about where they lived before I recruited 'em." The Captain winked at Sol.

"I see. They 'volunteered'."

"We were kidnapped," said Tom.

"See ya, Sol," said the Captain. "I gotta find me someone to race." He briskly pushed Tom ahead of him up the towpath. "Why cain't you behave like Sandy here?"

"Why don't you let us go?" asked Tom.

"Anybody want to race caterpillars?" yelled the Captain, instead of answering Tom's question.

"I'll race ya," called a captain from the deck of a green-painted laker. "Fleetfeet can beat any caterpillar hatched. Let me see yours."

Captain Reuben gently tilted the tobacco can and a smooth, white caterpillar with black and yellow stripes tumbled into his hand.

"There he is friend, put your money where your mouth is," said Captain Reuben.

"Wow, a Monarch," said Sandy.

"What?" said both captains.

"Sprinter is a Monarch butterfly caterpillar. We studied them in science class." She looked at the other caterpillar. "And that one's a woolly bear."

They walked over to a clear part of the towpath, followed by a growing crowd. A man trusted by both captains volunteered to be the referee. First, he drew a circle about three feet in diameter in the ground. The two captains checked it out and nodded that they were satisfied. Then he put a napkin ring in the exact center. The captains put their caterpillars into the napkin ring.

"Ladies and gentleman," spoke the referee, pretending that he was a ringmaster in a circus. "We have here a race between two mighty insects. The champion is Sprinter belonging to Captain Reuben of the 'Annie Lenore.' The challenger is Fleetfeet, belonging to Captain John of the 'Liberty Belle.' Finish making your bets. The race will commence shortly."

The crowd looked the two racers over carefully before making their choices. Men exchanged bets, and the two captains made a wager also. Sprinter began to climb out of the napkin ring, which caused more bets to be placed in his favor. The referee put Sprinter back inside, and announced the race.

"My friends, this race will be over when the first caterpillar crosses the circle. Its whole body must be outside the circle in order to be declared the winner. Part of the body doesn't count." He pulled up the napkin ring and shouted, "They're off."

Sprinter raised his head and seemed to be waiting for applause from the crowd. The crowd applauded, but it was for Fleetfeet, who was quickly making his way toward the circle. About halfway, he stopped and poked his head about carefully on the ground as if he had found a strange smell. Then he became motionless. Meanwhile, Sprinter had been slowly, but steadily, crawling toward the circle. When he passed Fleetfeet, the crowd went wild, urging each caterpillar forward.

"Go Sprinter," said Rebecca. "You can do it."

"Move those teeny legs," coaxed Tom who found himself caught up in the excitement.

"Put some gunpowder on 'em," shouted a spectator.

The noise from the crowd aroused Fleetfeet from his dreams. He moved very rapidly back to the center of the circle. His supporters groaned. Sprinter continued his determined course to the finish line. Fleetfeet was nearing the other side of the circle and got to it a little before Sprinter.

"Get ready to pay up, Reuben," said Captain John. "This race is over."

"Not yet," replied the Captain.

Instead of crossing the line, however, Fleetfeet began following the inside of the circle, as if the line drawn by the referee's finger was a bottomless crack in the earth.

"You numbskulled insect," shouted a man in the crowd.

Fleetfeet looked around as if offended. Sprinter's tail crossed the line and the race was over.

"The winner, and still champion is Sprinter," announced the referee. "Settle your bets like gentlemen and see you next time."

"Not sure there'll be a next time," said Captain John as he settled his bet with Captain Reuben. "Winter'll be here before you know it."

"Yep," said Captain Reuben. "Fair freightings to ya." The Captain picked up Sprinter and headed back to the boat.

"I told you Sprinter always wins," said Rebecca.

"Slow and steady wins the race," replied Sandy.

"Huh?"

"The story about the tortoise and the hare. You know, the hare's fast, but takes a nap. The tortoise just keeps going at a slow pace and finishes first."

"Where'd you hear that? I ain't never seen a rabbit and a turtle race."

"In a book, silly. You really haven't been to school much, have you? We'll start those reading lessons tonight."

# CHAPTER TEN

# POLLY'S PRESENT

"Captain," asked Ned as they returned to the boat. "Can I walk down a ways and see my gal? Her boat's tied up on the other side of the lock." He was dressed in clean clothes and had even combed his hair carefully.

"You look so spiffy, I cain't very well say no, can I? Go ahead, the young'uns and me can get through all right. We'll meet you at the end of the lock."

Ned bent down and picked up something green on the deck.

"He's got the bottle," whispered Sandy. Tom shot her a warning look and nodded toward Rebecca. "It's okay, Tom, I told Rebecca all about it. She's agreed to help us."

"Iffn you teach me to read."

"All right, but there goes the bottle. What are we going to do now?" said Tom.

The three children watched forlornly as Ned made his way to the top of the lock. Men stood by the heavy wooden balance beam which opened and closed the main lock gate. A hoggee was walking his team to the other side of the lock.

"Break up that mung meeting and hop to it. We're next," said the Captain. "Now, you two greenhorns, when those gates open on the lock, you unhitch the towrope and walk them mules up the path. Wait at the other end of the lock and I'll throw you the rope. Rebecca, git on board."

"Why don't we use the mules to pull the boat through?" asked Tom.

"Because the towrope would git all tangled up and the mules would end up in the water," said the Captain.

As the two lock gates were being opened, Tom untied the towrope and started up the path with Sandy walking by his side. The lock looked like a huge, stone-walled aquarium. He was amazed that only a few men could pull the boat into the lock.

"This is our big chance," said Sandy as they reached the end of the lock. "We can jump on the mules and ride out of here while they're busy."

"And do what?" replied Tom.

"Escape."

"Let me get this straight. We ride off down the towpath in a blaze of glory. Bad guys try to stop us, but we're too fast for them. As our thundering hooves leave our pursuers behind, I turn to the lovely damsel on the other mule. You smile at me with eyes full of gratitude. We get to town and ride up the courthouse steps. We tell the law that we're from the twentieth century and need to get a green bottle so that we can return to our regularly scheduled time slot."

"All right, Tom, stop. We're in a mess and I'm getting tired of it. I miss my family and my home. It may sound funny, but I have this craving for a nice thick peanut butter and jelly sandwich. I'm tired of all this fried food."

"I agree. It makes me sort of long for cafeteria food."

"I'm not that desperate," said Sandy.

"Okay, I didn't mean it," replied Tom. "But we're going to have to be patient and get that bottle."

"Rebecca said that she knows Ned's girlfriend pretty well. Maybe she can talk to her at the next lock."

"Speaking of Ned, here he comes," said Tom. Ned was puffing up the hill from the line of boats. His face was beaming happily.

"How do, young'uns? My gal liked that green bottle right fine. I"m so pleased I feel like singin', but don't worry, I ain't that cruel."

Tom stood up tall, put his right hand on his chest, and trying to sound like an opera singer, sang, "I've got a mule and her name is Sal, fifteen miles on the Erie Canal."

Ned looked puzzled. "I ain't never heard that one before."

"I thought that was the most famous Erie Canal song. You've really never heard it?" asked Tom.

"Nope, where'd you hear it?"

"In music class," said Sandy.

Ned scratched his head and looked at her inquiringly. Sandy and Tom didn't say anything more, so he took a piece of paper out of his pocket.

"Polly, my girlfriend, says that Sam Patch is gonna make another jump. Says this piece of paper tells about it. Could you read it for me? I wasn't too good in school."

"Sure," said Tom. "It says, 'HIGHER YET! Sam's Last Jump. Some things can be done as well as others. There's no Mistake in Sam Patch. Of the truth of this he will endeavour to convince the good people of

Rochester and its vicinity, next Friday, Nov. 13, at 2 o'clock P.M.'"

"What's this all about?" asked Tom.

"Why this Sam Patch fella jumps off of things. He gets a crowd, passes the hat, and then jumps off bridges or waterfalls. Why, he even jumped off Niagara Falls once. He's got a trained bear that jumps too. It must be a great sight."

"It's on Friday the 13th," said Sandy.

"I reckon that's right. Sam likes to be dramatic. Don't tell me you young'uns are superstitious," said Ned.

"No," said Tom. "But I'm not sure I'd risk jumping off waterfalls on that day."

"You wouldn't risk it any day," teased Sandy. "Does he really have a bear that jumps off waterfalls?"

"Yup. I heard that bear jumps right into the water and ain't scared of nothin'."

"Do you think that we'll be able to see it?"

"Sure. The Captain takes a shine to these things, and we'll make Rochester in plenty of time, unless there's a disaster."

"Tell us about Polly," said Sandy.

"Oh, she's about the perttiest cook on the canal. Her eyes are real blue, and she has curly red hair that shines in the sun. You can spot her from a fair distance by lookin' for her hair."

"Why Ned," teased Sandy. "You sound like you're in love."

"Yup, I reckon so. Soon as we save enough money, we're gonna buy our own canalboat and git married," said Ned.

"What's Polly's last name?" asked Tom. He figured that they were going to have to find her, so he was trying to get more information.

"Hollister," replied Ned.

"What is she doing now?" asked Tom.

"She cooks meals for Captain Isaac Lyon on 'The Genesee Gent.' Isaac hired her last season after his wife died. Some boats are run by families, like the McWilliams'. Sometimes, single men or widowers have to hire gals to cook for 'em."

"Don't men ever cook?" asked Sandy.

"Nope, it ain't seemly for a man to cook, but some poor men have to, I reckon," said Ned.

"That's terrible," said Sandy. She clenched her fists and her face tightened.

"Now, Sandy," soothed Tom. "Women's Lib hasn't been invented yet. A woman's place is in the kitchen, right Ned?"

"Course," said Ned.

"Rrrrr," growled Sandy. "You two are hopeless. I'm going back to the boat."

"I reckon we'd all better git back," said Ned. They led the mules and followed a few steps behind Sandy, who was storming ahead.

# CHAPTER ELEVEN

# Letters and Checkers

"Pa, Sandy's gonna teach me to read tonight," announced Rebecca. It was after supper and the crew members of the "Annie Lenore" were relaxing in the main cabin.

"I don't think that she can do it in one night," said the Captain. "Readin's kind of hard."

"I know, but I'm gonna learn fast. Iffn I do, I won't look so stupid in school."

"Reckon you'd better git started then, if they got their chores done," said the Captain.

"They're done," said Tom. "The mules are fed, brushed, and bedded down. All set for tomorrow."

"Then I'd be pleased if you could teach her." The Captain returned his attention to the checker game that he and Ned were playing on a small table.

"I've got somethin' from my schoolin' days that might come in handy. I've been savin' it for my children. I reckon now's the time," said Grizzy. She went to retrieve it from her trunk in the cuddy.

"That's great," said Sandy. She and Rebecca were seated at the small table that was used for meals. A metal oil lamp with a glass chimney cast a yellow light over the tabletop. "All right, Rebecca, I guess we'll start with the alphabet. Do you know any of the letters?"

"Some."

"Do you have some paper and a pencil?"

"A pencil?"

"Don't you know what a pencil is?" asked Tom.

"No, is it something that you learn about in school?"

"Oh, brother," said Tom as he rolled his eyes toward the ceiling.

"Shut up, Tom," shouted Sandy. "If you can't be nice, be quiet. Ignore him, Rebecca. Do you have anything to use for writing?"

"Why didn't you say so? I've been savin' wrapping paper for practicing my letters, and Pa bought me a pen and ink for my birthday so's I'd be ready for school. Will they do?" asked Rebecca.

"Sure, go get them," said Sandy. She wondered if perhaps pencils hadn't been invented yet. Rebecca met her mother as she was coming through the doorway.

"Here's the primer," said Grizzy.

"Thanks, Ma. Give it to Sandy. I'll be right back."

Rebecca disappeared behind the doorway. Grizzy gave the book to Sandy, who immediately opened the old-time schoolbook. On the inside cover was written a poem, which had been painfully copied in uneven script.

"What's this poem, Mrs. McWilliams? 'If this book should chance to roam, box it's ears and send it home. Griselda Harrison, age 7.' Did you write it?" asked Sandy.

"I forgot about that," Grizzy giggled. "Schoolbooks is valuable, so when we was in school, we wrote poems in them so's they wouldn't git lost."

"Did you make this one up?"

"Land sake, no. There was lots of poems that we learned from the older ones. Another that we used to write was 'Steal not this book, for if you do, Reuben

McWilliams will be after you.' Remember that one, Pa?" asked Grizzy.

"Yup," said the Captain. "I never did like school much, but we had some fun times in those days."

"Captain," said Tom. "When do you think we'll be in Rochester?"

"What are you worryin' about Rochester for?"

"Didn't Ned tell you about Sam Patch's jump?"

"Is that fool doin' it again?"

"Polly says he's gonna jump the Genesee Falls on the thirteenth. I told the young'uns that we'd probably be there about then," said Ned.

"Should make it," said the Captain. "It won't hurt to see the jump. We've only got this load of nails to take up to Buffalo and then we're done for the season. Don't think it's gonna freeze early with this warm spell we've been having."

Rebecca returned to the room with her materials and sat down at the table with Sandy, eager to begin the lesson.

"I'm going to pretend that you don't know anything about reading. That way I'll be able to teach you new things and review at the same time," said Sandy.

"You're lucky you don't have to take a whole week of standardized tests before you start," said Tom.

Sandy ignored him, and began printing each letter at the top of the paper. It was hard using the old-fashioned pen. The pen was similar to the kind that she had used in art class to make India ink drawings. Still, it was difficult to use the scratchy pen on the rough surface of the wrapping paper. While she was carefully forming each letter, she pronounced it and asked Rebecca to do the same. Each time that she made one letter, she had to dip the point into the ink again. It took about twenty minutes to get through the whole alphabet.

"Now that we've done all of the letters, I'm going to point to each one and you can tell me the names. Here we go."

Rebecca studied each letter carefully, often wrinkling her face in concentration. "A...B...C...D...ah, these next two look the same."

"Yes, they do," said Tom.

"Who's doing this lesson, you or me?" said Sandy.

"Okay, Teach. Don't get testy. I'll go sit in the corner." Tom moved his chair and watched the checker game.

"Can I play the winner?" Tom asked.

"Soon as I'm done whuppin' Ned, you can play 'im. I've got some harness to tend to," said the Captain. "In fact, I think it's over now." He moved one of his kings across the board, capturing the rest of Ned's pieces. "Good luck," he said as he got up and left the room.

Tom sat down and examined the checkerboard. The checkers were rough slices of corncob. Ned started placing his checkers, which were rubbed black with soot, on the board. Tom did the same, taking the ones with red dots painted in the centers. He listened to the reading lesson as he prepared for the game. "Sandy, you're a natural teacher. Mrs. Ferguson would be proud of you," he said.

She smiled and continued the lesson. Rebecca learned quickly, as if each letter was a new present to be opened on Christmas morning. Sandy repeated the letters patiently. At last she was satisfied. "That's enough for tonight. Tomorrow I'll show you some easy words. Right now I need to look over your mother's book."

"We appreciate your helpin' our girl," said Grizzy.

"It was fun," said Sandy as she began reading the primer.

"Mrs. McWilliams," said Tom. "When is school open around here?"

"Usually starts about the time the crops are in and everyone's pretty near ready for winter. Probably the winter term'll start in December."

"That's all?" asked Tom.

"There's a term in the summer, but Rebecca won't be goin' then because it's canal season."

Tom surveyed the checkerboard. Ned had done considerable damage while Tom had been talking. "Hmmmm. I can see that I'm going to have to concentrate more on the game. You've been sneakin' up on me."

"Bein' able to read don't mean your so all-fired smart," said Ned.

"Oh, I might be able to salvage this game," said Tom. He jumped two of Ned's pieces. Ned now had five pieces and Tom had three. Ned pulled on his suspenders and made his next move.

"Now you've done it," said Tom as he jumped two more pieces. "King me."

"Just a trap, young'un." Ned calmly jumped three of Tom's checkers and removed them from the board.

"I see you're a master. I'd better think more."

"Fine with me. I ain't gonna go easy on you," said Ned.

Tom studied the board carefully. It was clear that Ned had a plan for winning the game, but Tom couldn't figure it out. At home, he'd played a few times with his dad. He wished that he had played more checkers and watched less TV. He promised himself that he would try to get his dad to teach him some strategies when he got home. "Okay, Ned. I don't know what you're up to, but I guess I'll soon find out," he said as he moved a piece.

"You bet," said Ned as he wiped Tom's pieces off the checkerboard.

"I'm probably just tired," said Tom. "I'll beat you next time when I'm awake. Goodnight." He got up from the checkers game and started back to the bowstable. Sandy followed.

"Mind your manners, Rebecca," said Grizzy.

"Thank you, Sandy."

"You're welcome. Good night."

# CHAPTER TWELVE

# Breach

It was another brilliant autumn day. They were past Syracuse and were on their way to Rochester. Tom was doing his morning shift on the towpath. The weather had been unusually mild, which was fortunate because he had only a thin jacket. He hoped that these fine days would last until they could get home. He scanned the towpath up ahead. Coming toward him was a man riding a horse. His clean navy-blue pants and coat made him look more official than the other people that Tom had observed on the canal. He turned his horse and rode beside Tom.

"You seen any weak spots in this section, boy?" he said.

"What do you mean?"

"You know, muskrat holes, things like that."

"I'm sorry. I haven't worked on the canal for very long. Who are you?"

The man stiffened in his saddle. "I'm the pathmaster. I'm responsible for this stretch of canal. A fella up ahead said he saw some muskrats workin'. They dig holes and weaken the bank. I stuff them holes with straw so the canal don't breach."

"Breach?"

"Jeepers creepers, you are a greenhorn. Why a breach is when the bank gives way and the canal water drains out."

"Oh. Now that you mention it, I think I remember reading about that."

"Readin' about it?" The pathmaster shook his head. "Just be sure that you don't experience it. Keep your eyes peeled for any weak spots and tell any pathmaster about 'em."

"You mean there's more than one?"

"Yup. Each of us is in charge of about 25 miles of the canal. We're the sheriff and caretaker rolled into one."

"You mean you're the law here?"

"Yup."

"Maybe you could help me. My friend and I have been kidnapped."

"Yup. That's what hoggees say when they're tired of workin'. I imagine you want your wages for what you done, and then you want to skip out and buy whiskey."

"No, sir. I don't drink whiskey. I've been forced to work against my will."

"I don't see no gun at your back. Why don't you just leave? Go back home to wherever you're from. Where's that?"

"Niskayuna."

"Never heard of it. Indian name?"

"Yes. It's around Schenectady."

"Well, you've come a fair piece. You could have run away before this. Your folks mad at you?"

"I doubt if they even know that I'm gone."

"I think you're stretchin' the truth a bit, boy. Lots of boys run away and sign on a boat. Then they change their minds and blame the captain for makin' them keep their bargain. I can't help you unless you've got witnesses who seen you kidnapped. I'll bet you don't."

"No, Sandy and I were alone when they grabbed us. I guess we'll have to get out of this mess by ourselves."

"You ain't really in a mess. Workin' on the canal's not a bad life. Finish the season and then go home. It's good for a boy to finish what he starts. And meanwhile, keep an eye out for muskrats. Giddap."

The pathmaster turned his horse again and rode down the towpath. "Full freightings, Captain," he shouted as he passed the "Annie Lenore." Tom felt a bit foolish for telling the pathmaster that he had been kidnapped, but nothing had come of it. It was worth a try, he thought. I guess we're on our own.

A few hours later, he came to a spot where the towpath felt spongy. The mules' hooves sank a few inches and although they had difficulty, they got through it. I wonder if there's muskrat holes under there, he thought. As if to answer his question, he heard a trickling sound behind him.

He rode on the right side of the towpath and spotted a stream of water running through the bank.

"Captain, I think the canal's breaching," Tom yelled.

"Git those mules goin'. We gotta get as far away as possible."

Tom kicked Jupiter and quickly pulled the "Annie Lenore" away from the widening breach. Tom had never seen anything happen so quickly. In one moment the breach had gone from a small trickle to an ugly, swift torrent. The canal water was starting to empty into a farmer's cornfield.

The Captain was steering the "Annie Lenore" close to the bank so that they wouldn't be stranded in the middle of the canal if it drained. "Tom, unhitch Jupiter and ride up the towpath. Find the pathmaster and have 'im send the hurry-up boat. This breach is serious."

Tom did as he was told, glad to have other people giving orders during this emergency. Already an inch of wet bank was exposed, and the breach was getting worse. Tom climbed onto Jupiter's back and started up the towpath. He went as fast as he dared, afraid that he would slide off the mule's bare back. Mercifully, he only had to go a short distance before he met a pathmaster galloping toward him.

"There's a breach," shouted Tom.

"Where boy?"

"That way," Tom pointed back the way he had come.

"The Captain says it's serious and you should send something called a hurry-up boat."

"Ride up the path to Dingman's store. Tell the storekeeper to call Nelson Karner. Tell him to send the hurry-up boat toward Albany."

Tom tightened his grip on the mule's harness and sped up the towpath. He didn't mind riding at the normal pace, but galloping was too scary. The harness was not designed to be used as reins and kept sliding from side to side. Tom discovered that if he held on to both sides, he could steady it. Tom risked a peek ahead.

Lucky there's nobody on the towpath to run into, he thought. I just have to hold on a bit longer. After what seemed an eternity, he saw a small store up ahead.

# CHAPTER THIRTEEN

# Showing Off

Tom felt strangely comfortable when he entered the store. The warm tone of the wooden counter and the cluttered oak shelves gave the store a homey atmosphere not found in the brightly-lit, metal-and-plastic supermarkets at home. Sam Dingman, the storekeeper, was wrapping a package for a large woman with a black shawl. Two other women were waiting their turn in front of the long wooden counter. A ladder stood off to the right, so that Dingman could reach things on the higher shelves. In the dark corner, several men were sitting around a pot-bellied stove. The floorboards squeaked as Tom walked up to the counter.

"What do you want, boy?" asked Dingman.

"There's a breach back down the canal," said Tom. "The pathmaster says to send the hurry-up boat."

The men, who had been lounging around the woodstove, leaped up at the news. A short, powerfully built man with stringy hair and a beard came over to talk to Tom. There was concern in his eyes.

"Which way, boy?" he asked.

"Are you Nelson Karner?"

"I am. Where's the breach?"

"It's that way, toward Albany," said Tom.

"How far?"

"I don't know. It seemed like I rode forever."

"Let's go gents." The men, who had already put on their boots and coats, followed Karner outside. They reminded Tom of professional wrestlers, strong and stocky.

The storekeeper was staring at Tom, as if he was supposed to leave with the men, or buy something. There were jars lined up on the counter in front of him, each one filled with brightly-colored candy drops. He reached into his pocket and found some coins. I guess I won't need any ice cream money at the school cafeteria for a while, he thought. He must have put some in his pocket the other morning out of habit. There was no place to spend it on the field trip.

"How much are those orange drops?" he asked the storekeeper.

"Five for a penny."

"Great, I'll take five."

"Lemme see your money," said Dingman.

"I've got a penny."

"Well hand it over."

Tom handed Sam Dingman a penny, and then took off the lid to the jar that contained orange-colored candy.

"Not so fast, young'un," said Dingman as Tom reached into the jar. "This ain't no penny."

"What do you mean?" protested Tom. "Sure it is."

"Ain't even big enough for a half cent."

"Oh, I guess things are different now. Here's another penny," said Tom as he pulled out another coin from his pocket.

"Where do you come from, young'un? You talk peculiar, and them clothes ain't the kind we wear in these parts."

"I come from Schenectady."

"Don't they use Federal money in Schenectady yet?" asked Dingman.

"What?"

"Federal money. Made in the United States of America."

"Of course," said Tom. "Look on that penny. It says United States of America right on it."

"I reckon it does," said Dingman as he examined the coin. "It also says 1985. How do you explain that?"

Uh-oh, thought Tom. "I guess it was a mistake when they made it. Give it back and I'll be on my way.'

"Not so fast. Who's this fella?"

"That's Abraham Lincoln."

"Never heard of him," said Dingman. "He come from Schenectady too?"

"No. He was one of our best presidents. He freed the slaves. You don't know anything about history," sneered Tom. This was the first person that Tom had met that knew less about history than Tom.

"Don't you git sassy with me. I went to school for eight years and I know my presidents, Washington, Adams, Jefferson, Madison, Monroe, John Quincy Adams, and our new president, Andy Jackson himself."

"What about the Civil War?" asked Tom. There seemed to be no doubt that it was 1829.

"Why the War of 1812 is over. I never heard it called a civil war." Sam Dingman took a penny out of the old-time cash register and handed it to Tom. "This is what a penny looks like in these parts."

Tom picked it up and looked at it carefully. It was about the size of a modern quarter. One side had "ONE CENT" written in the middle of a wreath. The other side had the head of Liberty, and the date, 1827. Tom picked up his modern penny and compared the two. Okay, he thought, I'd better get out of here.

Tom put his penny back in his pocket and backed away from the counter toward the door. "I guess I won't be having any candy after all. It was nice talking to you," said Tom. "Good-by."

"Weak-brained hoggee," muttered Dingman as he shook his head in disgust.

When he reached the door, Tom felt for the knob, turned it, and stepped outside. He breathed a sigh of relief as he closed the door. Some of the men had just finished harnessing a team of horses. Others were checking equipment in the hurry-up boat. The hurry-up boat was actually a repair scow that was owned and operated by New York State.

At seventy feet long, it was eight feet shorter than the "Annie Lenore." The front and back ends sloped sharply up from the waterline, making it much faster than ordinary boats. Piled on the deck were shovels, axes, lanterns, large coils of rope and chain, and some tools that Tom couldn't identify. There was even a pile of dirt with an upside-down wheelbarrow laying on top. Men kept arriving to help, some climbing into the hurry-up boat, and others waiting on horseback, ready to ride down the towpath. The emergency preparations reminded Tom of the volunteer fire company in his town. When the fire siren wailed, men from all over town would swarm to the firehouse.

"Let's go," shouted Karner. The company of farmers and canalworkers took off like a small cavalry charge. By the time Tom had climbed onto Jupiter's back, the hurry-up boat was far ahead. He followed behind at a steady pace, not wanting to endure the galloping again. He wasn't sure that they would need him to help, anyway. The water level of the canal was a bit lower than before. I hope that this isn't going to prevent us from getting to Rochester on time, thought Tom.

As Tom approached the breach, he heard the activity of the workers. He was surprised that they weren't all standing around the hole in the canal, shovelling in dirt. Instead, the men had spread out and were performing different jobs. Some farmers were chopping down trees. A team of oxen was standing on the towpath, ready to drag the fallen trees into place across the breach. Nelson Karner was everywhere, urging the men to work faster, and moving them to a new job as soon as they had completed one.

Tom tied Jupiter's bridle to a small sapling in the woods along the towpath, and walked over to the water's edge. Sandy and Rebecca were watching the workmen from the deck of the "Annie Lenore."

"How long will it take to get it fixed?" called Tom.

"Oh, it'll take a while," answered Rebecca.

"I guess I'll go over and see if I can help," said Tom. He walked to where Ned and the Captain were working with three other men, straining to roll a tree into the breach.

"Can I help?" asked Tom.

"I doubt it," grunted Ned. "But give it a try."

Tom picked up an iron bar and jammed the tip under the log. The bar's weight surprised him. It was much heavier than it looked. The Captain checked to see if everyone was ready.

"On three, gents," ordered the Captain. "One, two, three, heave."

The log rolled forward as the men repositioned their bars after each push. Tom had to hurry to keep up. By the time he placed his bar under the log, the men had already rolled it ahead. Okay, Tom, he thought. Try harder and don't embarrass yourself in front of these men. He pushed the point of the iron bar along the ground so that it would be ready when the log stopped rolling. Using this plan, he was able to keep up and feel a sense of pride when the big log splashed into the canal, slowing the rush of water.

"No time to gloat," said the Captain. "Here comes another one."

Using the oxen, the farmers had dragged another log in position behind Tom's crew. Nelson Karner wanted to make a log dam over the breach and then fill in the cracks with straw and dirt. Later, other workmen would repair the damage permanently.

"I'm ready for the next one, Captain," said Tom.

"You done good, young'un. Let's git that other log," said the Captain.

Tom beamed and felt like he was a part of the crew, doing a man's work. I always get stupid jobs at home, he thought, boring stuff like emptying the wastebaskets or cleaning my room. This is real work, he thought. He put his iron bar under the log and waited for the signal to push.

"One, two, three, heave." The log started rolling and Tom kept up by sliding his bar as he had before. They stopped just short of the breach and waited for the other workers to receive it.

"Are you ladies ready for this log or not?" asked the Captain.

"Be patient, Reuben. You ain't goin' anywheres until this breach is fixed," said a workman named Abe.

"Go to, Abe. We'll just set here and pass the time."

Since no more trees were needed, the farmers began returning home. John Miller, the owner of the field into which the canal water had drained, was complaining to Nelson Karner, trying to get some money from the Canal Commission to pay for the damage.

"Been nothin' but trouble since Clinton and his gang built this dang thing," said Miller. "My corn crop's ruint."

"It's November, John. You should have gotten your corn in a month ago. Write a letter to the Canal Commission anyway, and maybe they'll pay for your crop," said Karner. He walked away to help with the loading of the tools.

"We'll take that log now, Reuben. If it's convenient," said Abe.

"At your service," said the Captain as he made a sweeping bow to the workers.

Tom picked up the heavy iron bar and pushed the point under the log. He looked up the canal and saw that Sandy and Rebecca were watching him. Okay, he thought, I'll show those girls how a real man handles work. He straightened his back and expanded his chest a bit. He considered spitting into each hand, but decided that he didn't want to be too much of a showoff. He concentrated on his bar so that he would look like an important worker.

"Drop her in, boys," said the Captain. "One, two, three, heave."

Tom pushed the bar as hard as he could, but instead of moving the log, he drove the point of the bar into the soft earth. It hit a rock, causing him to lose his balance. The end of the bar gashed his neck as he fell down.

# CHAPTER FOURTEEN

# First Aid

Tom lay still on the ground, feeling like a deflated beachball. The wound on his neck was throbbing. Nearby, he heard the log being secured, and saw a fuzzy shape appear above him.

"You've a nasty scrape there, young'un," said the Captain. He knelt beside Tom and examined the wound. "We'd better git you back on board the 'Annie Lenore'. Can you walk?"

"I don't know. Maybe if you help me," said Tom. The Captain pulled him up and put his arm around Tom's shoulder. Tom felt weak and dizzy as they walked slowly back to the "Annie Lenore." Sandy was anxiously waiting for them.

"Are you all right?" she asked.

"Don't worry about it," snarled Tom, feeling embarrassed because he had been hurt trying to show off.

"Come on. Anybody could have an accident."

"Can you take care of him?" asked the Captain. "I've got to get back to the breach and help finish up. Grizzy's up the towpath jawin' with the women. I'll send for her."

"I'll take good care of him," said Sandy. "Here, Tom, I'll help you down the steps."

The Captain started to say something, changed his mind, and started back to the breach.

Tom and Sandy descended the steps into the kitchen. Tom felt weaker than before, and was leaning heavily on Sandy. At the bottom of the steps, he collapsed onto the floor.

"Okay, Tom. I'm going to help you. Just relax."

"What do you know?" groaned Tom.

"I had a first aid course at 4H camp. I probably know more about medicine than these people do."

"Just leave me alone."

"Tom, don't be stupid. You're bleeding and probably in shock. I know just what to do," said Sandy.

"Okay, do your worst. I'm too dizzy to argue."

"First, let's get your shirt off and stop the bleeding. No, that's not right. The book said I'm supposed to treat for shock before anything else. First, you must lie down."

"I'm collapsed on the floor. Are you sure you know what you're doing?"

"Of course. At camp, we pretended we were on the scene of a tragic airplane crash. There were kids everywhere, pretending to be bodies. First, I elevate the victim's feet to keep a steady flow of blood to his head."

"There's enough blood in my head. Why don't you stop it from bleeding?"

"All in good time." She put the washtub under Tom's feet.

"Next, we must keep the victim warm by covering him with a blanket." Sandy found comfort by following the routine that she had learned in camp. It helped to keep her calm.

"I'm not a victim. I just cut myself."

"Shock is serious. You're a trauma victim. Now lie still." She went to the back cuddy and got a blanket from Rebecca's bed.

"There, I put a blanket over the victim," said Sandy.

"I'M NOT A VICTIM!"

"Okay, patient. Take it easy. The patient must remain calm."

"What's going on here?" asked Grizzy as she entered the cabin.

"I'm treating him for shock," replied Sandy proudly. "I know first aid."

"Mercy. This is no time to play doctor. He's bleedin' and we've got to wash that neck. Sit up, boy."

"At last," said Tom.

"Sandy, go to the canal and fetch me some water. Git that shirt off, Tom. Land sakes, I never saw such folderol over a cut."

"Sandy likes to be dramatic," said Tom.

Sandy returned with the bucket of water. Grizzy dipped a cloth into it and began washing Tom's neck.

"You didn't sterilize the water. He'll get infected," yelled Sandy. "That water's dirty."

"Water's water. Now hush up," said Grizzy. "Git up on deck and do something useful instead of botherin' me."

Later, Tom was sitting on the roof of the bowstable, watching Sandy on the towpath. His neck felt better, although the bandage bothered him when he swallowed. His larynx moved up and down against the cloth. I hope that when I get back home, this cut stays in 1829, Tom thought.

"Are you feeling better?" asked Rebecca as she joined him.

"Yeah, but this bandage feels like a noose."

"I'm sorry that you got hurt. How did it happen?"

"My bar hit a rock."

"Sandy sure knows a lot about doctorin'."

"What? I was laying there bleeding and all she did was smother me with blankets," said Tom. "Your mom is the one that helped me."

"Sandy says that you needed to keep warm and quiet. She explained it all to me. I think she'll make a good doctor someday. You should be thankful for all the things that she done to help you."

"But I was bleeding."

"Oh, stop bellyachin' about your bleedin'. You should appreciate Sandy's wantin' to care for you," said Rebecca.

"Okay. Okay. I appreciate it. Can we change the subject? When are we going to get to Rochester?"

"Pa says we oughta be there by tomorrow morning. That will get us there in plenty of time to see Sam Patch."

"And find Ned's girlfriend."

"I still don't get this. Sandy says that you and her live 150 years from now, but here you are in my time. And this is called travellin' in time. Do folks do this alot?"

"No, it only happens in stories. Everybody thinks that time travel is only make believe."

"Well, what are you gonna tell folks when you get back?" asked Rebecca.

"I really haven't thought about it. In the stories, the hero usually comes back at the same time he left, so nobody knows he was gone. Maybe I won't have to say anything. I'll get a great mark on my Erie Canal report, though."

"It's real hard talkin' to you. Everytime you talk, I have a question."

"I don't mind."

"Then what's an Erie Canal report?"

Tom laughed, causing Rebecca to blush. Her face hardened. "I'm sorry. In my school, the teacher made us read a bunch of books about the Erie Canal. Then we had to write about it in our own words. I was studying about how the locks work."

"That's easy. Water fills 'em up and then they drain out."

"I know, but in my time, kids don't get chances to see a lock, so we have to study them," said Tom.

"And you read about us in books?"

"Yeah, how about that? People like your Pa get their pictures in history books. Maybe you will too."

"Imagine bein' in books."

"Rebecca," called Grizzy. "Time to fix supper."

"Comin' Ma," replied Rebecca. "I gotta go. Hope your neck feels better."

"Thanks," said Tom. "Good luck with your reading lessons tonight. Be a good student."

"I'll try," said Rebecca as she left the bowstable roof.

# CHAPTER FIFTEEN

# Dr. Evans' Cure

"How's that cut, boy?" asked the Captain. They were eating breakfast in the cabin on Friday morning, the thirteenth of November. Tom hadn't slept very well and felt feverish. His swollen wound made the bandage around his neck too tight.

"It hurts some, sir," answered Tom. He was pushing the greasy potatoes and eggs around his plate. "I don't feel much like eating."

"Let me take a look at it," said Grizzy. "Move over to the light."

Tom dragged his chair into the doorway of the cabin and sat down. Grizzy began to unwrap the bandage, which stuck fast to the wound. It hurt as she pulled it away.

"It looks poorly," she said.

"Let me see," said Sandy as she looked over Grizzy's shoulder. "It's infected," she said. "Look at it oozing."

"Sandy, don't be gross," said Tom.

"Well it is. Isn't there a doctor that can fix it?"

"She's right, Pa," said Grizzy. "I think we'd better have a doctor look at this."

"All right," said the Captain. "I reckon we could find a doctor somewheres between here and Rochester. We'll be at Richardson's tavern before long. I'll ask Elias where we can find one. Sandy, I guess you'll have to work the towpath this morning. Don't look like Tom here's gonna make his shift."

"I don't mind."

"Thanks, Sandy. I appreciate you're helping me. I'm sorry if I acted like a jerk yesterday."

"Yesterday wasn't the only time that you acted like a jerk, but it's okay. You get some rest."

"I will. I'm going back to sleep right now." Tom got up and headed for the bowstable. It was a cold day with threatening rainclouds overhead. He was glad when he could flop down on the straw bed, for he felt weak and had walked slowly. At first, he laid on his side, propping his head up with his right arm. He stared at the mules' hooves and listened to their slow, never-ending munching. A mouse appeared in the middle of the floor and started nibbling on a seed that had fallen from a feedbag.

"Hi, Ralph," whispered Tom. The mouse froze and looked at him. Since he had read *The Mouse and the Motorcycle*, he called every mouse that he saw "Ralph," not that he saw too many. "Could you get me an aspirin for my fever?" He remembered the part of the book where Ralph had run all over the hotel to find Keith an aspirin for his fever. The mouse scurried away. "I guess you didn't read the book," said Tom as he rolled over and went to sleep.

The Captain gave a blast on his tin trumpet, signalling Sandy to halt. She got down from Comet's back and held the team next to the stone wall of a low bridge. Across the canal was a two-storied building which was painted a color similar to a golden-yellow schoolbus. The Captain steered the "Annie Lenore" behind a packet boat that was tied up to a small dock a few feet past the low bridge. Sandy looked across the canal at the tavern. Men in suits were smoking cigars on the second floor porch, leaning back in their chairs with their feet on the ladder-like railing.

"You hold the mules steady," the Captain ordered Sandy. "I'm gonna ask about a doctor over at the tavern." He walked across the bridge and into the tavern. Because of the cold, gray weather, the patrons were noisily roaming about the crowded main room. The Captain walked around the tables of men playing cards or checkers, looking through the clouds of tobacco smoke for Elias Richardson, the innkeeper.

He spotted him behind the bar, talking with some canal workers.

"What'll it be, Reuben?" asked Elias when the Captain approached the bar. The innkeeper was a bit chubby, with whiskers that made a "W" on his face.

"Just information, Elias," replied the Captain. "I got a sick hoggee that needs doctorin'. Are there any around these parts?"

"Yes, there's Doc Evans a few miles up the towpath in Pittsford. Lives in a big white house with green shutters right by the canal. Sure you don't want to wet your whistle while you're here?"

"I think I will have a short glass of rum," said the Captain. "It'll warm me on this miserable day."

"Goin' to see the jump?"

"I reckon. You think that fool Sam Patch'll make it?" asked the Captain as he downed his drink in one swallow.

"Never know. That's what makes it interestin'. I got a copy of yesterday's newspaper, want to see it?"

"Indeed I do. I've got some young'un's back on my boat. Could I take this along so they could read it? They'd be mighty interested."

"Sure, it's a day old anyways."

"Much obliged," said the Captain. He paid and headed out the door. Even though the day was cold and damp, he was glad to be in the fresh air. He never liked crowded, smoke-filled rooms. I guess that's why I work on the canal, he thought as he walked back to the "Annie Lenore."

"Tom, wake up," said Sandy. "We're at the doctor's house."

"Are you sure that this is a good idea? Before I fell asleep, I remembered reading about old-time doctors. Suppose he amputates my head?"

"Not a bad idea."

"Come on, Sandy. I'm scared."

"Okay, he'll probably just clean the wound with antiseptic and give you a new bandage. Now get up."

A few minutes later, Sandy, Tom and Grizzy were walking toward the porch of a white clapboard house with green shutters. There was a small sign to the left of the doorway that said, "John B. Evans, Doctor of Medicine. Please knock."

"Now don't fret, Tom," said Grizzy. She knocked on the front door and stepped back. Instantly the door opened and a man in a faded blue suit appeared.

"Saw you comin'," said the doctor. "Got a cut, young'un?" Dr. Evans reminded Tom of the pictures that he'd seen of Abraham Lincoln. He was tall and thin, with dark hair and a beard. His kind eyes helped ease Tom's fear.

"The boy here scratched hisself back a ways," said Grizzy. "I washed and bandaged it, but it's not mending properly."

"Come in and I'll take a look," said the doctor. He led them to his office, which was the front room of his house. It was sparsely decorated, with a wooden floor and whitewashed walls. On one wall was a chart with different drawings of the human body on it. Dr. Evans pointed to a table and took a pair of scissors out of a cabinet. Tom climbed upon the examining table, dangling his legs over the side. He gasped when he saw the doctor come toward him with the scissors.

"I'm just gonna cut away this bandage, son. No need to be frightened. Lie down."

"I knew that," said Tom, but he didn't relax any as the doctor began to cut away the bandage. "That hurts."

"I know. Be brave. I'm almost done." The doctor pulled the remaining cloth from the wound. "Yup. You've got a nice infection there. Didn't you wash it?"

"She used that filthy canal water," said Sandy.

"I see. Well, a few leeches will get rid of the swelling. Then we'll......"

"Leeches!" Tom sat upright. "No way."

"Lie down, boy. They don't hurt." Dr. Evans took a forceps and pulled the worm-like creature out of a jar.

"Just look at this beauty." He held up the pale-green leech. It was a few inches long, with brown stripes running the length of it's segmented body. The wiggling body dripped water on Tom's arm.

"Get that thing away from me!" Tom shouted. He began kicking his feet on the table. "Get me out of this century. I'm not afraid to die. Just don't let that thing near me."

"Grab his feet," said the doctor. The Captain's wife and Sandy each held down one of Tom's legs while Dr. Evans leaned over Tom's chest and arms. Carefully, he put the leech's head on the cut. The leech held fast with its sucker mouth. Dr. Evans pulled another leech from the jar and placed it on the opposite side of the wound.

"Now boy, I want you to lie still. The leeches need time to suck the infection out of that cut. Does it hurt?"

"Not really. It feels like you put two little vacuum cleaners on my neck."

"Two what?"

"Never mind. I'll be calm now."

"Good. You just lie here for a few minutes. Your friend can stay with you while I speak with Mrs. McWilliams in the next room. Call if you need me."

After they had left the room, Sandy came over to the table and stood by Tom. She felt sympathy for him. It had been hard enough for both of them during the past few days without being injured as well. She decided to try to cheer him up.

"The leeches seem to be reducing the swelling, Tom. Does it hurt much?"

"They feel gross on my neck, but it doesn't hurt. I guess I made a fuss over nothing."

"I bet I would have screamed my head off too," said Sandy. "You've had a tough time."

"Yeah. I don't want to sound mushy or anything, but I'm glad that you are the one that came with me instead of those other airheads like Darlene or Cynthia. You've been a big help."

"Thanks," said Sandy. "I wonder if we'll ever see those creeps again. It would sort of be nice to look into their plastic faces."

"Yeah, but only for a few seconds."

"Right. Are you going to feel well enough to help me find the bottle today?"

"I hope so," said Tom. "I'm tired of the boring towpath. Did the Captain say when we'd get to Rochester?"

"It's only a few miles from the doctor's office. I've been thinking that we should stick together from now on. I don't know if the bottle has anything to do with time travel or not, but if it does, we should both be near it. Otherwise, one of us might be stuck here forever."

"That makes sense. You know, I always thought that girls were useless. I've changed my mind."

"Good," said Sandy. "You were a real blockhead in the beginning, but you're improving."

"What's that paper you're holding?" asked Tom.

"Oh, I almost forgot. The Captain got us a newspaper with an article about Sam Patch. Want me to read it?"

"Sure," said Tom.

HIGHER YET!
SAM'S LAST JUMP!
"SOME THINGS CAN BE DONE AS WELL AS OTHERS."
"THERE IS NO MISTAKE IN SAM PATCH."

"That's the same as that other paper that Ned had," said Tom.

"That's right," replied Sandy.  She read more.

"OF THE TRUTH OF THIS HE WILL ENDEAVOR to convince the good people of Rochester, and its vicinity, next FRIDAY, Nov. 13, 2'clock, P.M. Being determined to astonish the natives of the West before he returns to the Jarsey's, he will have a scaffold Twenty-Five Feet in height erected on the brink of the Genesee Falls, in this village, from which he will fearlessly leap into the abyss below—a distance of ONE HUNDRED and TWENTY-FIVE FEET.

"SAM'S BEAR, (at 3 o'clock precisely) will make the same jump and follow his master, thus showing, conclusively, that 'Some Things can be done as well as others.'  Moreover, Sam hopes that all the good people who attend this astonishing exhibition will contribute something towards remunerating him for the seemingly hazardous experiment."*

"What's that last sentence mean?" asked Tom.

"That Patch expects the people to give him money for risking his neck.  Feelin' better?" asked Dr. Evans as he entered the room.  He walked over to Tom and examined the wound.  "Looks like most of the swelling's

89

gone.  I'll just take my friends off your neck and you may go."

He took a salt shaker and sprinkled salt on the leeches.  "These fellas don't like salt," explained Dr. Evans.  "They let go because it hurts their skin."  The leeches dropped from Tom's neck and landed on the table.  The doctor took the forceps, picked them up, and returned them to the jar.  After washing it with antiseptic, he  wrapped Tom's neck with a new cloth bandage.

"You're all set.  Take care."

"Thank you," said Tom.

* The Rochester Historical Society Publication Fund Series, Rochester, NY 1937, Vol XII, page 187.

# CHAPTER SIXTEEN

# At the Genesee Falls

"Time to go," the Captain called down the cabin stairs. Ned and Sandy had just finished helping him stable the mules and tie up the "Annie Lenore." Tom was eating some soup at the table while the Captain's wife and daughter were getting dressed in the cuddy.

"We're a'comin'," replied Grizzy as she and Rebecca emerged from behind the blanket-door. Rebecca was wearing the red-checked dress that Tom had worn while his clothes were drying on the first day of his capture. Her mother was clothed in a somber grey dress with a white lace collar at the throat. The hem of the long skirt brushed against the toes of her black shoes. She had a black shawl wrapped about her shoulders, and carried an umbrella in case of rain. Although she still wasn't smiling, Grizzy appeared more friendly in her "Sunday best" outfit.

"You two look great," said Tom. Rebecca smiled and Grizzy grunted. He left his soup bowl on the table and followed them up to the deck.

The "Annie Lenore" was tied up behind a long line of canalboats that had also come to Rochester to see Sam Patch make his leap. The Captain, Grizzy, and Ned walked up the towpath toward State Street, followed by the three children. Most of the people had already left the boats so that they could get a good view of the falls for the jump.

"I hope Polly waited for me," said Ned. "I hadn't planned on bein' this late."

"The breach held us up some," said the Captain, "but we'll find her. It's only about 1:30. We've got a half-hour before he jumps."

About ten minutes later they came to the aqueduct that crossed the Genesee River. They stopped on the aqueduct to look northward, where farther downstream the river went over a steep cliff on its way to Lake Ontario. The scattered buildings along the river gave no hint that someday Rochester would be a major city in New York State.

"Better not dawdle," said Grizzy. They crossed the aqueduct and came at last to State Street, which led to the falls.

"Yoo-hoo," called a voice. Standing on the deck of a blue and white canalboat named "The Genesee Gent" was an attractive woman with curly red hair and a warm smile. She was wearing a bright blue dress in the same style as Grizzy's. "I thought you'd never get here."

"Hello, Polly," said Ned. "We got mudlarked a ways back and had to help fix a breach. You already know the Captain and his missus."

"Sure do," said Polly. "How are you folks doin'? And here's Rebecca."

After the McWilliams' greeted her, Ned introduced her to Tom and Sandy.

"You're lucky to be workin' for such fine people." Polly's eyes twinkled and made Tom feel like she was his friend, even though he'd only known her for a minute.

"Pleased to meet you," said Sandy. "Ned has told us so much about you." Polly blushed and smiled at Ned, who blushed also. It was easy to see that they were in love.

"Yes, he has," said Tom. "How do you like that green bottle he gave you?"

"I like it fine," said Polly. "I put it on my dresser so's I can think of my Ned whenever I see it."

"Sounds romantic all right," said Tom. "Can I see where it is? Sandy and I have a special interest in it."

"There's no time, boy," said the Captain. "Let's git goin'."

Tom looked at Sandy and shrugged, as if to say "I had to try." They walked down a short hill and up the level street toward the falls. There were a few groups of people far ahead, but none behind. Tom lingered a bit, studying "The Genesee Gent" to make sure that he would recognize it when he and Sandy returned. When he was satisfied, he followed the adults in silence. He felt stronger than he had earlier, but was still a bit weak from the infection. He passed the time imagining the moment when he would see his parents again. He had never missed them more than when he was lying on his straw mattress last night burning up with fever. You always want your parents when you're sick, he thought.

Soon they arrived at the upper falls of the Genesee River. The falls spilled into a huge bowl that had been carved out by the river's currents. The sides of the bowl

93

were vertical cliffs of crumbling grey shale, the same color as the cloudy sky above. Tom was impressed. The water had created a cavern behind the falls, so that a person could fit between the roaring river and the cliff. A few feet from the State Street bank of the river rose a small rock island that parted the cascading water like a finger. Sam Patch would jump from a platform that had been built on this island. A narrow wood-plank bridge spanned the short distance between the platform base and the riverbank.

Several thousand people lined the rim of the rock bowl, talking excitedly, drinking from small pocket-sized whiskey bottles, and placing bets. Many of the women had umbrellas. Tom and Sandy worked their way through the crowd toward a good spot where they could see the jump and also make a fast get-away when it was over. When they got to the edge, they could hear the roar of the falls for the first time, the sound no longer concealed by the noisy crowd.

"Okay, Sandy," whispered Tom. "As soon as he hits the water we make a run for it. The crowd will be excited and no one will notice."

"Aye, aye, Captain," teased Sandy. She saw the pained look on Tom's face. "I'm sorry. Just an old habit. Do you feel strong enough to make it?"

"I'll make it. I feel like my life depends on it. I'll rest tonight in my own bed."

"What do you think it will be like when we get back?" asked Sandy.

"In all of the stories I've read, the time-traveller comes back at the exact moment he left. I'll probably be cured and arguing with you about the bottle, or swatting the trees with a stick."

"I hope that's the way it is. I don't want to have to explain this," said Sandy. "It'll be our secret."

"Fine with me," replied Tom, "Only I can't wait for the Erie Canal test at school. After what we've learned here, I might even get a perfect paper. My parents will freak out."

The crowd began to get restless, for it was past two o'clock and Sam Patch had not appeared. Shouts of "Where's Patch?" and "Come on out, you chicken" were heard amongst the impatient spectators. Tom looked at the tower to see if anything was happening. He and Sandy had gotten close enough so that they had a good view of everything. He wished that Patch would get it over with so that he could get home. As if to grant his wish, a small man appeared, dressed in white tight-fitting pants and shirt. He had a black scarf tied around his waist. The crowd cheered as he made his way across the bridge, followed by a few men. A black bear followed Patch on a leash. The bear seemed unafraid, but Patch was walking unsteadily. I'd be scared too, thought Tom.

Several men were passing through the crowd asking for money to reward Sam Patch for his leap. One of the men thrust a hat with a few coins in it at Tom and Sandy. When Tom shook his head no, the man grunted, "Hoggees never have any money anyways." He moved on to a more prosperous looking gentleman.

Sam Patch tied the bear to the base of the tower, and began to climb the fourteen-foot ladder to the top. The noisy crowd urged him onward. When he reached the top, Patch looked over the crowd and then down at the bear. The bear gave a sad roar, which set the crowd to cheering again. Sam then walked over to the edge and stared into the pool that swirled 110 feet below him. He quickly returned to the center of the platform. Tom couldn't see his face too well, but he had the impression that all was not well with Sam Patch. The crowd sensed it also and began to call him names again.

At last Sam took off his scarf and waved it to the crowd, which became much quieter. He retied the scarf around his waist, and then raised his arm.

"Napoleon was a great man and a great general," he said in a shaky voice. "He conquered armies and he conquered nations. Wellington was a great man and a great soldier. He conquered armies and he conquered Napoleon. But he could not jump the Genesee Falls. That was left for me to do. I can do it, and I will." *

"He's really going to do it," said Sandy. "I didn't think he would."

"He's got no choice," said Tom. "This crowd will hang him if he doesn't."

* Adams, Samuel Hopkins. *Grandfather Stories.* Random House, New York, 1955, p. 264. Many of the facts of Sam Patch's leap come from the chapter of this book entitled "Sam Patch's Fearsome Leap."

# CHAPTER SEVENTEEN

# Sam's Leap

"Where do you think you're sneakin' off to?"

Tom's heart thumped and Sandy gasped as they turned around to find Rebecca right behind them.

"Oh, Rebecca," said Sandy as she caught her breath. "You gave me a scare. I thought it was your Pa."

"Do I sound like my Pa?" asked Rebecca, "Or are you two jumpy because you're tryin' to sneak off?"

"Okay, you're right," said Tom. "We're leaving after the jump."

"You can't leave now," cried Rebecca. "I'm only beginnin' to get the hang of readin'."

"Oh, Rebecca," said Sandy. "You're a smart girl. You don't need me. You'll learn this winter in school, I'm sure of it."

"Please stay until we get to Buffalo," pleaded Rebecca. "I'll help you get the bottle then. I'll even sneak into Polly's cuddy. And I won't care if I get caught."

"No, Rebecca," said Tom. "I want to go home now. My neck hurts and I still don't feel that good."

"Besides," said Sandy, "Suppose the bottle breaks or Polly pulls out the cork? Maybe she'll go to our time. We'll be stuck here forever and Ned would lose his girlfriend. Don't you see? We have to get back to our parents now. It might be our last chance."

"Look," said Tom. "He's going to jump."

The crowd quieted while Sam walked to the edge. He held his arms tightly to his side and looked into the pool again. He took a step backwards and relaxed his body. "Come on, Patch. Git it over with," yelled a man close to Tom.

Sam went to the edge again, holding onto the railing. He closed his eyes, gave a yell, and jumped into the air. At first, Sam shot straight as an arrow toward the pool below, but soon he lost control of his body. His arms and legs doggie-paddled in the air. Before he could straighten out, he hit the water with a big slash. The crowd gasped and rushed as close to the edge as they dared, looking for Sam to bob up and wave. Tom and Sandy peered over the edge, but only saw the swirling water.

"It's time," said Sandy. "Good-bye, Rebecca. It's been nice knowing you and your family. Good luck at school." She felt a bit sad as she walked away.

"I won't forget you," said Rebecca.

"Good-bye," said Tom. "We won't forget you either. Please don't tell on us." He turned away and followed Sandy through the crowd.

They rushed away before Rebecca had a chance to answer. "I won't tell," she called as she stood forlornly and watched them disappear. I wonder if that fool story about them comin' from the future is true, she thought. Maybe they'll be waitin' at the towpath when we get back. She turned and hunted for her parents.

"Did he make it?" asked a small girl who was far back in the crowd.

"I don't know," said Tom.

Sandy was about ten feet ahead of Tom when they got out of the crowd. "Slow down," called Tom. "I have to make it the whole half mile."

"Sorry," replied Sandy. "Why don't you lean on me?"

"Not yet, but I'll ask for help when I need it."

"Tom, you have changed. You are finally able to ask for help. I'm proud of you."

"Oh, stop. Let's get going." Tom felt embarrassed, but pleased.

They walked together silently and met no one for the entire length of State Street. Tom was thinking of home, trying to push himself forward. He felt tired and the walk back to the canal was a struggle for him. Sandy was thinking about the past week. She really would miss the people she had met, and the uniqueness of being in a different time. Being there was certainly more interesting than reading about the canal, although she loved to read. She promised herself that she would keep the bottle and return again to 1829. When they came to the little hill that led up to the canal, Tom was feeling tired.

"Okay, Sandy. I need some help now."

He put his right arm over Sandy's shoulder and together they walked up the hill to the towpath.

"There's the boat," said Tom. He found a spot on the path that was free of manure and sat down. "Can you go in and get the bottle while I rest on the towpath? You can call me if you need help."

"Okay. Warn me if anyone comes."

Sandy went aboard "The Genesee Gent" and walked nervously to the aft cabin. She felt like a thief on some TV show, hurrying to grab the jewels before the police arrived to arrest her. She took a deep breath and concentrated on getting home. When she got to the cabin door, she found a padlock through the rusty hasp. Great, she thought, now we'll never get home.

"Tom," she yelled, "It's locked!"

"What?" Tom called back in disbelief. "You mean we did all this for nothing?"

Sandy came to the side rail of the canalboat. "Can you think of another way in?"

Tom looked over the outside of the cabin. "Try the windows."

Sandy ran to the first blue-shuttered window and lifted it up. It wasn't locked, but the window sash stuck when it was opened only two inches. Sandy tugged and strained, but it wouldn't budge.

"Hurry up," called Tom. He never had been very patient, but now he was bursting with frustration. Sandy ran to the next window. She pulled it up with all of her strength, willing it to open far enough for her to enter the cabin. The window slid easily and she crawled through. She felt around with her foot for something to stand on, and discovered that the eating table was under the window. She eased both of her feet onto the table. Her foot struck something that rolled off of the table and shattered on the floor.

"Now you've broken the bottle," shouted Tom. He got up from the towpath and walked toward the canalboat.

"It's okay," said Sandy. "It was just a jar of flowers. Stop yelling at me, I'm nervous enough. I don't think that I'm cut out to rob people."

"I'm sorry. You're doing fine. Hurry up, though, I'm going crazy out here."

The cabin was exactly the same in design as the "Annie Lenore's", but seemed neater and more brightly decorated. The walls were whitewashed, which made them appear cleaner than the dingy yellow of the "Annie Lenore." Polly had made blue stripped curtains for the windows, and hung some brown-toned pictures of rigid-looking people on the walls. Dried flowers were scattered on the floor, as were pieces of the broken jar. Sandy stepped over the glass and went to the cuddy doorway. She pushed a solid yellow blanket that served as the door to her left and entered the room. The bottle was on the dresser, just as Polly had said.

"Sandy," Tom yelled from outside. She ran out of the cuddy and climbed up on the table, imagining fifty canalboat captains with guns waiting for her. She peeked out the window. There was only Tom standing on the towpath.

"What now?" Her voice shook with anger and fear.

"Did you find it yet?" asked Tom.

"Yes, and I was just about to grab it when you called. I thought that someone was coming."

"Sorry."

"Stop saying you're sorry and let me get the bottle," scolded Sandy. She climbed down from the table and returned to the cuddy. She quickly located Polly's dresser with the green bottle standing proudly on the top. The cork was still in the neck. She grabbed the bottle, ran across the cabin, and crawled out of the window.

"Be careful," called Tom, "or you'll break it."

Sandy held the bottle tighter as she walked toward Tom.

"Here it is," said Sandy. "You certainly didn't make it any easier for me. I was nervous too, you know."

"I'm sorry. It was hard to wait out here." Tom looked all worn out from worry.

"Forget it. Do you think that Sam Patch made it?"

"We'll look it up when we get home," said Tom. "Let's do it!"

Sandy held the bottle tightly in her arms, and Tom closed his thumb and two fingers around the cork.

"You've been great, Sandy," said Tom. "I'm sorry that I was a jerk and I just wanted to say that before we get back."

"Just pull the cork," Sandy blushed. Tom tightened his fingers and pulled the cork out of the bottle.

# CHAPTER EIGHTEEN

# Home At Last?

"Hey you kids, get out of the way," yelled a man from the passenger window of a red van. A loud horn blared near Sandy's ear as the light turned green and the van roared through the intersection.

"Sandy, I don't think we're with our class on the field trip," said Tom as they both retreated to the curb. They were standing on the corner of a wide, modern street. Trucks, cars, and a lone bicyclist raced past them. Behind them, the clock on the glass and metal bank announced the time of 3:02 in pale green letters.

"We came back at the right time, but this isn't the right place," said Sandy. "Do you know where we are?"

"Yup," said Tom, "We're in Rochester."

"Okay, genius, how do you know that?"

"There's a police car parked across the street in front of the newspaper building. What does it say on the door?"

"Rochester Police," said Sandy.

"You've solved the case again, Ms. Encyclopedia Jenkins."

"And look, the street next to us is called 'State Street!'" said Sandy. They looked around the corner and saw that the little hill was still there. "So we're back in modern times, but at the exact spot where we were standing in 1829. This street," she looked at the street sign, "Uh, Broad Street, must have been the old Erie Canal. What are we going to do now?"

"I don't know, but I'm never going to trust time-travel stories again. They said that we'd be back at the same place and time that we left."

"Tom, they're just stories," said Sandy.

"I know, but it would have been nice to be where we belonged instead of here. Should we ask the policeman for help?" asked Tom.

"I guess so. What are we going to tell him?"

"Not the truth," said Tom. "I've got it. Captain McWilliams thought we were runaways, let's pretend we are. Let's tell them we hitchhiked to Rochester, but we miss our families and want to go home."

"Sounds good to me. Let's go," said Sandy.

They waited for the traffic light to turn green and crossed State Street, and then Broad Street. One officer was sitting in the blue and white car. The door had a golden eagle perched on top of a circle that had "Rochester Police" written on it. Inside the circle was the number of the police car, 132. Tom stuck his head into the open window.

"Hi, kid," said the officer. "Where did you get that nasty cut?" Tom felt his neck and discovered that the bandage was still there.

"Uh, we, I mean, my friend and I ran away from home and we've changed our minds and want to go back. Could you help us call our parents. We don't have any money."

"Where do you live?"

"Near Schenectady. We hitchhiked, Officer Gomez," Tom read the name tag on the officer's uniform.

"Why'd you run away?" asked Gomez.

Sandy stuck her head into the window and spoke. "Please help us. It's all my fault. I had a fight with my parents and needed someone to run away with. Tom got hit by a trucker and his neck hurts. Can you help us?"

"Okay," said Gomez. "Hop in the back seat."

"Do you know anything about a man named Sam Patch?" asked Sandy as she climbed into the car. Tom got in after her and closed the door. Sandy put the bottle on the seat between them. Officer Gomez started the car and drove down the street.

"Yes, I do," said Gomez. "He was a fella that jumped off the Genesee Falls a long time ago. You can still see the place where he jumped if you walk over the footbridge a few blocks behind us."

"Did he make it?" asked Tom.

"Nope. They found his body frozen in a cake of ice near Lake Ontario. I think he jumped around Thanksgiving and they found him around St. Patrick's Day. Something like that. Must have been quite a sight."

"It was," said Sandy, "I mean yes, it must have been something. Did he have a bear?"

"Yes, the bear used to jump too. Bruin, that was his name, disappeared after Sam Patch jumped. No one knows what happened to him. You kids like history?"

"I didn't before," said Tom, "but lately I've been getting more interested in it."

"Get your parents to take you to the Strong Museum. It's got lots of neat historical stuff. Well, here we are," said Gomez as he pulled up in front of the police station. "Come with me. I have to report this to the Captain."

"Oh, no," chuckled Tom, "Another captain."

"Huh?" asked Gomez.

"Never mind," said Tom.

They walked into the police station. Officer Gomez led them to a wooden door with a large glass window upon which was painted "Captain Robert McWilliams, RPD." Sandy pointed to the name and Tom nodded his head as they followed Gomez into the office.

A female officer wearing a police uniform was sitting behind a desk, interviewing a well-dressed businessman.

"Is the Captain free?" asked Gomez.

"Yup. Go on in," replied the officer.

The Captain's office was small, but extremely neat, just like the Captain. He was dressed in a blue suit that had no wrinkles. His black hair was cut short, and not a hair was out of place. Gomez explained Tom and Sandy's story to him, and then left the room. The Captain motioned with his hand that they were supposed to sit down in the chairs in front of his desk.

"You two sure smell," he said as he sniffed the air. "When was the last time you took a bath?"

"About 150 years ago," said Sandy.

"Smart, huh? I hate smart-mouthed kids."

"Sorry," said Sandy. "It was just a joke. Can you please let us call our parents?"

"Just a few more questions. What's in that bottle?"

"Nothing," said Tom. "She found it on the street."

"Let me see it," demanded the Captain.

"No," shouted Sandy as she wrapped both arms tightly around the bottle and pressed it to her chest.

"You want to go home? You give me that bottle, now!"

"Go ahead, Sandy. Let him see it. It's just a dirty old bottle," said Tom.

"Okay, but don't pull out the cork. I don't want to lose it." She set the bottle on the desk. The Captain picked it up and looked at it closely.

"You kids trying to hide something?" he asked as he continued to examine the bottle.

"No sir," said Tom. "By the way, do you know anything about the Erie Canal?" He thought that he could distract the Captain with a question.

"Not much," said the Captain as he put the bottle back on the desk. "One of my ancestors had a boat on the canal, but I only know his name."

"What was his name?" asked Sandy.

"Reuben McWilliams," he said as he picked up the bottle again. "What are you kids trying to hide?" His fingers reached for the cork.

"Don't do that!" yelled Sandy.

"Why not?"

"It's poison," she said.

"Nice try, kid," said the Captain as he pulled the cork out of the bottle. His body blurred a bit, and then disappeared. The bottle was gone as well.

"Full freightings, Captain," said Tom. "I hope that you like your relatives." He looked over at Sandy who was staring at the wall behind the desk. "Come on, let's go make some phone calls."

He stood up, pulled Sandy out of the chair, and together they walked out of the room.

*THE END*